Also from Second Wind Publishing
Novels by Lazarus Barnhill

*Lacey Takes a Holiday*

*The Medicine People*

www.secondwindpublishing.com

# Come Home to Me, Child

By

## Sally Jones and Lazarus Barnhill

Dagger Books
Published by Second Wind Publishing, LLC.
Kernersville

Dagger Books
Second Wind Publishing, LLC
931-B South Main Street, Box 145
Kernersville, NC 27284

First Dagger Books edition published
July 2012.
Dagger Books, Running Angel, and all production design are trademarks of Second Wind Publishing, used under license.

For information regarding bulk purchases of this book, digital purchase and special discounts, please contact the publisher at
www.secondwindpublishing.com

Cover design by Tracy Beltran

Manufactured in the United States of America
ISBN 978-1-938101-23-6

To Doris & Harvey, thanks for the inspiration.

# Chapter 1

"What's wrong with the gazebo where it is?"

Elaine shuddered. She glanced over her shoulder in the direction of the stranger's voice, her mouth open, her eyes wide.

"Oh, sorry. Did I startle you?" He was wearing the light brown uniform of a police officer, smiling casually, his hands in his pockets. "Guess I should have introduced myself first."

He was already too close to her and drew even closer as he reached out. For an instant she only stared at him, still trying to gather herself. She felt his hand, firm and powerful, grasp hers.

"I'm Larry Daughtry, the Chief of Police." He let go and stepped back. Lifting a thumb in the direction of the simple, one-story house whose backyard bordered hers, he grinned boyishly. "I'm also your neighbor."

At last she was able to respond. "Hello. My name is Elaine—"

"Elaine Randolph." The police chief completed her sentence. "And you and your family just moved here from Dallas."

"Well, Richardson."

"Same difference to me. All big city." He put his hands back in his pockets. "Welcome to Veil, the best hometown in North Texas."

"Th-thank you, Mr. . . . ."

"Daughtry. Larry Daughtry. Most folks call me 'Chief'. But since we're neighbors, why don't you call me 'Larry'?"

Elaine struggled to recall the little ritual she had been taught by her physical therapist. When flustered, it was okay to close her eyes, take a deep breath and say something about what she felt right then.

"You just surprised me, Mr. Daughtry." She opened her eyes. "I didn't realize anyone else was here. I was talking with our contractor, Mr.—"

"Tim Starling!" The chief interrupted her again. He stepped around her and punched the smaller, quiet man on the shoulder playfully. "Oh, Tim and I know each other very well. We go way back. How long we been knowing each other, son?"

Starling shook his head, annoyed at the intrusion. "Don't get me to lying."

"Well, we graduated high school together over at Blue Ridge."

Elaine had calmed enough to study the chief more carefully. He wore the tan of a person who spent hours outside every day. His thinning, yellow hair and mustache were pale against his weathered face. And he was strongly built. Not as tall as her husband Jim, but thicker. Muscled.

"Mr. Starling is going to move our gazebo."

"Yeah, that's what I overheard." The chief grasped one of the thick timbers of the shelter. "I'm sort of attached to it, really. I guess Tim told you he was the builder who constructed it originally?"

"Yes."

"Well did he tell you I helped him?" His voice had a conspiratorial tone. "I was glad to help the Blanchard's. They were great neighbors." He faced her and smiled. "'Course you and Jim will be too, I'm sure."

"I'm sorry," Elaine said. "You—you have the better of me. You seem to know all about us."

He hung his head in mock humility. "Well, it's only gossip, Miss Randolph. In a town no bigger than Veil, new people moving in makes everybody curious—especially when they're going to be your new neighbors. When Janet, your realtor—"

"Mrs. Thomason?"

"Yeah. When she put the 'sold' sign in the yard, my wife Sheila and I came right out and started quizzing her about you all. I suspect she didn't tell us anymore than is public record."

"Well, we don't have any big secrets, Sheriff."

"'Chief,' ma'am. I understand your husband is a big executive downtown."

She nodded. "He's the Vice-President of Sales for DCC, a wholesale supply company."

"Yes, ma'am. And I understand he's keeping his job in Dallas and commuting every day?"

Elaine sighed. "Yes."

"Quite a drive. And you have two young kids, right?"

"Yes. Our son Jake is almost sixteen. He'll be a junior when school starts. And Camille, our daughter, is—" She stopped, her mind suddenly completely blank. "—I'm sorry. Sometimes my memory plays tricks on me."

"That's quite all right, ma'am." For an instant the chief seemed truly sincere. "I believe Janet said she's going to be in the sixth grade."

"That's right. Eleven. She's eleven."

"Sheila and I have a daughter ourselves. Well, that's the rumor. We don't see her much anymore now that she's twenty-four. Her name's Susan. She has an apartment in Bedford and works at DFW. We only see her when she runs out of groceries before the end of the month."

"I see." Elaine smiled. He seemed a bit more human to her as he talked about his child.

"So." He pounded his hand against the upright timber again. "How come you're moving the old gazebo?"

"Puttin' in a hot tub," Starling said.

"Oh?"

"It's a therapeutic spa for me," Elaine said slowly. "I'm recovering from some surgery on my brain, which can take a long time. This spa is part of my treatment."

"Well, while recognizing it ain't my business," the chief said, "do you mind me asking why you don't just put the tub on the far side and leave the gazebo where it is?"

"I'd have to dig under it anyway to run the plumbing," Starling explained, looking down. "There's not much to digging under the footings, bringing it back fifteen feet, setting it in and bringing it to level. Then we'll build a low deck around the new site for the tub. Having the hot tub closer to the house makes it easier for Mrs. Randolph to get into and out of the water. Plus it offers a little more privacy. When we get it in place, we'll put a fortress fence around the backyard."

"Fence? Oh!" Daughtry acquired a surprised, chastened expression. "Well, Miss Randolph, just speaking from a nosy policeman's point of view, it sure does make it more difficult to spy on your neighbors when they have a fence."

They all laughed.

"Speaking of policing, I got to get to work. It's nice to meet you and you're in good hands with my old buddy Tim here. He really is a good contractor, for a guy who played the trombone. If you ever have an emergency or you need anything—you or anyone in your family—I'm here to protect and serve."

"Nice—nice to meet you, Chief Daughtry," she stammered.

"Please do call me 'Larry,' ma'am."

He turned and walked away, hands in his pockets. It seemed to her that he made no noise as he moved. She couldn't hear him leaving any more than she heard him come up behind her.

Elaine glanced toward Starling. "Trombone player?"

He smiled, shaking his head. "You aren't from Texas I take it, Mrs. Randolph?"

"California originally."

"Well in Texas, all high school boys are divided into two groups: those who play football and those who don't. Those footballers like Larry, who was a nose tackle on defense and a tight end on offense, are accorded a special distinction of 'near sainthood'. I liked music and I played in the marching band." He began making notes again on the pad that held a large diagram of the backyard. "Actually I was all-district band three years in a row. And—" He pulled out his tape measure. "—when I went out to Commerce, to East Texas State, to study drafting and construction, I played in the marching band there as well."

Her gaze followed Daughtry, who had disappeared through the row of cedars shielding his house from theirs.

"What about the chief?"

"He went into the Marines. Became a military policeman or shore patrol—whatever they call 'em. Did three or four hitches and came back to work in law enforcement around here. He started as a Cochran County deputy and, about five years ago when the chief's spot came open in Veil, he was the natural choice. I guess."

"He seemed happier to see you than you were to see him."

Starling chuckled. "I always thought Larry was a kind of a thug. He bullied me. Not that he was the only one." He began to stretch his tape measure along the yard. "It's the divine right of football players to torment band guys."

"Why was he so concerned that we were going to move the gazebo? We have the building permit."

"Well." Starling shook his head. "It's your gazebo. You can do what you want with it." He let the tape slide back with a snap and wrote a series of numbers on the paper. "I didn't realize this hot tub was for health reasons, Mrs. Randolph."

"Oh. My children think it's going to be for them. But actually its main purpose is to help me get better. I haven't always been this way, Mr. Starling."

"What way?"

"You're kind. I haven't always stuttered and lost words and gotten flustered at little things."

"You had a brain tumor, did you?" He pulled the tape out again, setting it perpendicular to the point of his previous set of measurements.

"Not a tumor. An aneurysm."

"Oh, yes." He began to write again. "I heard of those. A ballooning blood vessel."

"Yes. I never—never knew I had it. Until the day it burst."

"You're lucky to be alive."

"Yes."

"Would you mind?" He handed her the end of the tape. "Stand right there and hold this." He backed away from the house and the tape made a little gurgling sound as he pulled it. "My Uncle Horace died with an aneurysm."

"I was in the hospital. Already, I mean. I'm a nurse. I was a nurse, anyway. I was what they call a 'med-surg' nurse."

"Uh huh. Ma'am, would you hold the end to the edge of that post?"

"Okay. And I was feeling so strange. . . . I said to my friend . . ."

He was in front of her suddenly, gently taking the tape from her hand. "Are you all right, Mrs. Randolph?"

She gazed at his face, seeing the genuine concern in his eyes. She was inside the gazebo, sitting on a wooden bench. "How long?"

"Mmm. Five or ten seconds, I suppose."

"Oh. That's not so bad." She straightened herself. The light-headed feeling and the confusion melted away much more quickly than in the past and she remembered exactly what she had been talking about. "Did I tell you about Marci?"

"Who?"

"My friend. We were working together that day on my last shift. I turned to her and said, 'The room is turning left and blue.'" She laughed. "Isn't that funny? 'The room is turning left and blue.' That's the last thing I remember. My next true memory was in the

ICU and I had been there two weeks. I collapsed and they took me right away. If I had been anywhere else, I would've died. I had eight hours of surgery. They shaved my head."

He had stopped taking measurements and closed his notepad. His expression sober, he stood listening to her.

"Well, at first they just shaved where they went in. Later they shaved it all to keep an EEG running on me." She smiled. "They kept waving at my brain to see if it would wave back."

". . . You lived. You got well."

"Mostly. I had to learn to walk and talk. And feed myself. I didn't get home from rehabilitation for six weeks after the surgery. Most of my mental abilities have come back at least part way. The worst part is not knowing sometimes if I'm awake or dreaming." She gazed around inside the gazebo. "Can we just sit here and rest for a minute, Mr. Starling?"

"Of course." He sat across from her. "I have pretty much what I need. I guess I didn't realize this was part of your recovery process. We'll get it finished just as quickly as we can."

"You know," she said, "this whole move is supposed to be therapy for me. My neurologist told my husband I needed to get away from the city. He said I needed a quiet, restful environment where things were stable and there wouldn't be a lot of excitement. He said we should find the most boring place we could."

"Well that's Veil. You've succeeded in following your doctor's orders."

"Ha. Jim—my husband—has been so wonderful about this. So have my children. We haven't sold our house in Richardson. We leased it out for a year. Furnished. My kids will go to Veil schools for a year. Jim will commute sixty miles each way five days a week for a year." She shrugged. "I sure hope I get better."

"If I don't miss my guess," the contractor said, "watching you continue to recover will be all it takes to make their sacrifice worthwhile."

She smiled. "You're very kind, Mr. Starling."

He stood. "Well, this afternoon one of the guys on my crew, Antonio, will come over and dig around the footings of the gazebo. We need to see what shape they're in and exactly how hard it will be to move them."

"Okay. Antonio, right? I'll be watching for him."

"Is there anything you need help with before I leave? Anything you need carried or moved?"

"Oh, thank you. No. It's actually time for my afternoon medication and nap. When I wake up from that, Jim will be here with my kids and we can start putting away all the boxes the movers brought in last night."

He leaned against one of the gazebo posts. "You know, this will work out okay for you all. I know you've had to give up your life in Richardson for a year, but a lot of good things will happen for you. The economy is bound to keep getting better. These changes to your property—the new deck and built in hot tub, the fence—all these things will increase the value of this house for when you sell it." He straightened. "Okay then. Tomorrow we'll start by lifting up the gazebo and setting it yonder. Everything will be over in a week."

"Did they have a daughter, Mom?"

Elaine sat on the unmade bed in Camille's new room. "I don't know much about the Blanchard's, sweetie. This room is so feminine, though, it makes me think they must have a girl about your age."

"I wonder if she had friends around here? If there are more girls my age?"

"Don't know. Maybe we'll find out in the next few days. Do you like this lavender okay? I know you prefer yellow. We can paint it."

Camille walked away from the box of clothes she was unpacking and sat down beside her mother. "This is weird, Mom. I hope you don't mind me saying this."

"You can say anything you want, Cammie."

Her face grew dark. "I had to leave all my friends. And tell them, 'Well, I'll be back. Maybe.' So now I'm here in Veil and I'd like to make new friends. Only, in a year or so I may have to give them up too."

Elaine nodded. "It is unfair, isn't it?" She toyed with her daughter's long auburn hair. "I don't know how to make it up to you."

Camille set her jaw. "How about a pony?"

"Ha! That's my girl. I think you have to run that one by your dad. He's in charge of horses and all other livestock."

7

"Like kittens?"

"All that. Have you noticed your brother is strangely quiet?"

"The Jakester?" He didn't unpack much. Last I saw he set up his Xbox and was playing some disgusting game. He plugged in his ear buds so no one would hear it but him. And so he wouldn't hear anybody"

"Ah, teenage boys. Maybe I should go encourage him to finish putting away his stuff."

"What's for supper, Mom?" she called as Elaine walked out of the corner bedroom.

"'Dad's Surprise'." She replied. "I have no idea. Are there any restaurants in this burg?"

She padded toward the other end of the "L" shaped house, through the kitchen and living room and down the hall toward the other two bedrooms. Elaine stood in front of her son's closed door.

"Jake." When he did not answer, as she had anticipated he would not, she tapped on the door. "Jacob James.... All right. You asked for it."

She pushed the door open. He was listening to his iPod and stuffing clothes into his large, old chest of drawers. With his signature yank, he pulled the ear buds out with a single tug.

"*Ola, Mammacita. Como esta?*"

"Mammacita is okay. Are you making progress?"

"Yeah. I've been thinking."

"Every time you think, son, it costs me money."

"Oh, Mom." He flopped on his bed, putting his hands behind his head between the first and second bounce. "You want me to get acclimated here in Hicksville, right."

She tipped her head warily to one side.

"Just saying. I'm going to need a whole new wardrobe. You know, bib overalls, tacky western shirts with pearl buttons. Probably some suede work boots. We'll get those at the 'Cowboy Consignment Shop.' That way they'll already have cow manure stains."

"I can see now you're gonna fit right in."

"I'll give it my best, Mom"

"People do not like smart aleck strangers making fun of them."

"Ah, Mom!" He covered his ears in mock annoyance. "Dad already gave me this speech."

"Do tell? And what did he say?"

"He said I couldn't make fun of anybody either to their face or behind their back. He said I couldn't ju-jitsu anybody no matter how much they asked for it. He said if you two get a call from the police or the principal, you're automatically not on my side."

"Well it sounds like he's covered most of the bases."

Jake sighed. "He said we're going home this weekend for Gram Lou's birthday."

"It is her birthday, isn't it? I don't know what kind of present we can get her out here."

"He said he might let me practice driving when we get to her house."

Elaine pulled the chair away from his desk and sat on it. "I'm sorry, son. I should be letting you drive every day."

"I know, Mom. And the thing is, this is a much better place to learn to drive. It's not like North Dallas or Central Expressway. There is no traffic. No crazy drivers. Well, except for all the tractors on the road."

She smiled at him. "We'll be back in Richardson before long. Maybe that's where you should be practicing on the streets."

"I'm adaptable. Just give me the key and I'm booking." He caught her eyes, suddenly sincere. "I am a good driver, you know."

From somewhere in the direction of the kitchen, Jim Randolph's voice called out. "Dad is home! He's got pizza."

"All right!" Jake leapt off his bed and shot out the bedroom door.

Elaine followed him. "Wonderful teenager."

Jim sat two large flat boxes and two two-liter soda bottles on the table. Packing paper flew around him as he dug inside the boxes stacked by the cupboards. Watching his form—tall, lean, still youthful—made Elaine feel a bit more like an invalid. And guilty that she had not unpacked the dishes, even though he had told her to leave them alone.

"Plates coming," Jim said. "Glasses coming. . . . Get your own ice."

"Thanks, Jim."

"You're welcome. Have the kids got all their stuff put away?"

She slid into a chair at the kitchen table. "They got started. They have good attitudes."

9

"Well I guess that ought to be worth something. You want pepperoni and mushroom or supreme or both?"

"One of each, please."

"Coming up." He plopped a stoneware saucer in front of her with two slices of pizza on it.

"This is not bad," Jake said.

"Is there a napkin?" Camille waved her fingers as if they were on fire. "It's a little greasy."

"Here, kid," her father said. "Explain to your brother what these are for."

"That's what jeans are for," Jake mumbled around his pepperoni.

"I have a question," Jim continued. "This little town has one pizza parlor, one hamburger joint, one greasy spoon diner and three Mexican restaurants. What's up with that?"

"Dad, would you fill up my glass?" Camille asked. "I like burritos."

"You remember, Jim, when we lived in California and you applied for that job up in Marin County ten or eleven years ago?"

"Sure."

"Remember remarking about how that little town had one fast food place, one American bistro and four Thai restaurants?"

"Ah! You're right I do. I guess every place has its own special weirdness."

"That was California," Jake said. "California is supposed to be weird. Texas is supposed to be old-school."

Elaine took a drink and set her glass on the table. "I meant to tell you I met our next door neighbor."

"You mean the cop? Sandy headed guy with a mustache. A couple inches shorter than me?"

It startled her. "You met him too?"

"Well, actually he pulled up alongside me when I was leaving the pizza place. I'm opening the door and this police car eases up beside me. The passenger window rolls down and the driver says, 'Hi, Jim!'"

She nodded. "That's Larry Daughtry all right."

"My first thought was that something happened to you and they called an ambulance and they sent this guy to find me."

"I'm fine, dear."

"Yes, I know. Anyway, this guy parks, gets out and comes

around. He tells me he's our neighbor and if we need anything, we shouldn't hesitate to ask."

She gazed at him, waiting for him to continue. "So? What'd you think?"

"What'd I think? Seems like a nice enough guy. Why? Don't you like him?"

"You know, I can't say what it is exactly, but somehow the chief makes me feel a little uncomfortable."

"Is that why you had a spell?" Camille asked.

"Oh," Jim said, "was it a bad one?"

Elaine shrugged. "It was only five or ten seconds. I was talking to Mr. Starling, the contractor. He caught me and set me down in the gazebo." She frowned at Camille. "What are you, the seizure police?"

"What did Larry Daughtry have to do with it?"

"Oh, nothing, hon. I mean, I had just been talking to him. I think it had to do with me being on my feet all morning and standing outside for half-an-hour talking to Tim. I just overdid it."

Jim looked at her skeptically. "Well . . . why did you say that about Daughtry making you uncomfortable?"

"He was just real nosy, is all. Well, first he just seemed to appear out of nowhere. And he just inserted himself into my conversation with Tim Starling and took over. And he seemed to know everything about us: where you worked, how many kids we have, how old they are."

"That's cop skills for you," Jake said, his mouth full.

"That's our realtor," Elaine replied. "When Janet put out the 'sold' sign, apparently Daughtry and his wife Sheila saw her and asked her about us."

Jim shrugged. "Sounds like he has what it takes to make a good police officer."

"Suppose he does that with all new Veil residents?" she asked. "You know, just to let us know that we're being watched. Maybe it's his way of telling us to mind our P's and Q's."

"Or what?" Jim asked.

"Or they burn a pile of cow shit in your front yard."

"Jake!"

"Daddy, Mom told me today I could have a kitten."

"Cammie! What's wrong with you two? I told you to ask your

11

dad. I didn't make you any promises."

"Mom's promises don't count anyway," Jake said casually. "She's not right in the head."

"I'm right enough to confiscate your Xbox, smart guy."

The teenager grinned. "Oops! Did I say that out loud? I must have an aneurysm."

"Cammie," Jim said, "if I wouldn't let you have a cat in Richardson, why would I let you have a cat in Veil?"

"Not a cat. A kitten."

"Kittens have a way of becoming cats."

"Not if you're lucky."

"This doesn't concern you, Jake."

"Come on, Daddy. We're out in the country."

"We're in a subdivision, missy."

"Cats are not just pets around here anyway," Jake persisted.

"Oh really." His father's voice was testy. "And what are they?"

"They serve a purpose out here on the frontier. You know. They're meant for keeping down mice. And for target practice."

"Oh, Jake!"

Jim shook his head. "He's just saying that to get a rise out of you, missy."

Elaine began to laugh aloud. The others stopped eating and talking and turned to her.

"Are you okay, E?"

"Yes, yes I am." She sighed and smiled. "I spent most of the morning worrying about whether or not we would ever have a normal family day here in Veil. And I shouldn't have. This is just like being back home."


She sat on the edge of the bed listening to Jim's peaceful snoring and trying to assure herself she was truly awake.

Nights like this one were the worst for her. The dreams could be so incredibly vivid, as well as macabre and full of anxiety. Waking up offered little relief to her because of the hallucinations that often attended her unfinished dreams, breaking into her consciousness, as a doctor had explained it. It was only when she was awake in broad daylight she was truly aware of what was happening around her.

The medicine helped. The act of simply getting out of bed and going to the kitchen for a glass of water and opening the pill bottle often helped her shake the dreams and illusions. It was the desire of that small comfort that caused her to stand, unsteady at first, and walk quietly out of the bedroom. The clock glowed "2:30" in pale crimson.

In anticipation of a night like this, she had strategically placed night lights throughout the little house, glowing breadcrumbs intended to lead her to the kitchen and back in this new, unfamiliar place without tripping over something and hurting herself or waking her family.

As she walked through the dining room with its large plate glass windows, she glanced out at the backyard. In the moonless night, the only thing obvious to her was the dark outline of the gazebo. Then, it seemed, something in the gazebo moved.

Elaine stopped inadvertently. She heard herself draw a surprised breath. Shaking her head, she closed her eyes. Hallucinations. She glanced back, expecting to see only the straight, rigid lines of the wooden structure. Instead she saw again the moving shadow.

The dark form was not in the gazebo, but rather behind it. Entranced, she watched the shadow moving rhythmically. This was a mind trick to end all tricks. The gazebo was morphing into a living thing, looking like some great insect emerging from a cocoon. She could make no sense of the repeated motions she saw, until the shadow splintered, a long, thin branch standing apart.

"A handle," she whispered. "A broom—no a shovel handle." She felt herself smile. "I'm dreaming that Antonio came back. He's digging around the foundation again."

The flowing shadow disappeared. Elaine stepped toward the plate glass.

"There. You see. All in my head."

Just as suddenly, the shadow appeared again—only half as tall as before and not behind the gazebo, but to one side of it. Smoothly the shadow grew and remained still. It had assumed the shape of a man.

Elaine stared at it. She knew this shape. She recognized it from somewhere. Whose shadow was it? And then the thought dawned upon her that the dark form was either staring at her or standing with its back to her, looking in the opposite direction. And it occurred to her that she was not engulfed in darkness. If the figure in the backyard was actually a person, it could clearly see her watching it in the dull nightlights of the dining room.

She shivered, embarrassed and impatient at the illusion. Crossing her arms over her chest, she continued into the kitchen. The pill bottle cap made a satisfying pop as she thumbed it off. She dropped the pill onto her tongue and washed it down with lukewarm tap water and started back to her bed.

Passing through the dining room, she stopped to make sure the shadow was gone. There was a slight movement in the far corner of her vision. Something disappeared through the cedars that marked the edge of the Daughtry's property.

That was the familiar outline. It was the police chief whose shadow had been by her gazebo.

# Chapter 2

Elaine made her way slowly around the gazebo, studying it without a real awareness of what she was seeking. Where the six corners of the structure met the ground, she could see that Antonio had spaded up the earth. She glanced at the bay windows facing the backyard. From outside the house it was difficult to tell exactly where she had been standing in the dining room the night before.

Moving to the corner of the gazebo nearest the Daughtry's home, she gazed back at her dining room windows again. Yes, someone standing where she stood now would be visible clearly to someone in the house. And, standing inside the large windows, she would have been visible to the person by the gazebo as well.

She looked down at the earth around the gazebo. There was the dirt Antonio had turned. But why so much? She gazed at the other two corners of the foundation visible to her. Why was the exploratory hole so much larger at the corner right before her?

There were creases in the redwood base of the gazebo as well, the sort of little grooves that come from pressing a shovel handle up against a wooden frame while digging beneath it. Antonio had been careless.

She walked toward another of the excavated corners. Antonio left no marks on it. Hands on hip and head down, she walked all the way around the structure. The only shovel marks on the wood were at the point where, she believed, she saw Police Chief Larry Daughtry in the darkness.

"Mom!" It was Camille, shouting from the open living room door toward the backyard twice as loudly as necessary, startling her. "The nurse is here."

She gave her daughter a tight smile. "There's nothing wrong with my hearing, Cammie."

"Your nurse is here."

"Yes, thank you."

"She's in the entry hall thingy."

"I'm headed that way right now." She looked over the gazebo

15

again as she made her way to the door.

Standing in the entry, a thick bag hanging from her shoulder, was a petite, professional looking woman in her late forties or early fifties. She wore jeans and a jacket that seemed just a bit too large for her thin frame.

"Hello." Elaine held out her hand.

"Hi, Mrs. Randolph. I'm Julie Johnson. I'm your home health nurse."

"It is so nice to meet you. I'm so glad you're here. Can you call me 'Elaine'?"

"Sure."

"Want some tea or coffee?" She started in the direction of the kitchen.

The nurse followed her. "No, I just finished a large latte. I'm going to have to pee before I leave for sure." They laughed. "But thanks. If we can just sit at your table, I have to get some information."

"Sure. This is the one relatively orderly room in the whole house."

Elaine pulled out a chair and eased into it. The nurse sat beside her and unzipped a pouch on the outside of her bag. She produced a tablet computer and held down a button on its edge.

"Gone are the days of the two-inch thick paper files. At last. I love this little thing."

"Oh. Well if all your files are on the computer, what's all the rest of the stuff in the bag?"

She arched her eyebrows. "Stethoscope. Glucose monitor. Blood pressure cuff. Good old nurse stuff. . . . Here you are. . . . Okay. Are you Elaine Randolph? Age forty-one? Married? Former nurse—hey, cool! Two kids?"

"Yeah, that's me. Why are you—"

"Because I have a case load of about twenty-five people and I don't want to treat one when I think I'm treating someone else." She looked up from her screen. "One time I was meeting two new clients the same day. Miss Morrison and Mrs. Mercer. I test the first patient and say, 'Good news, ma'am! Your blood sugar is perfect.' She says, 'That's great. Only I'm not diabetic. I have congestive heart failure!' Ever since then, I make sure to really get to know my clients from the start."

"I was in med-surg. Hard to get to know those patients. Once they're well enough to talk, you're shipping them out to the floors."

"Really. I never did that, except during my initial rotations. I was trauma and ER before I went with home health care."

"The great thing about a clinical setting is when you get a little turned around about who you're working with, you just look at that little band on their wrist. Not that we still didn't make mistakes."

Julie began pulling equipment out of her bag and setting it on the table. "Do you miss it?"

"Oh. I haven't been gone from it long enough to miss it. And I've been so focused on getting back as much as I can. I've been told I'll never have enough function to be a nurse again."

"You have to wonder if that's a good thing or a bad thing." Her voice was casual. "If you don't have the capability to be a nurse, maybe you can at least be a doctor."

They chuckled.

Elaine studied her colleague. "So why did you choose home health care?"

". . . Well. The money's good. Don't have to wear scrubs, if I don't want to. Don't have to put up with some twenty-nine-year-old resident ordering me around and saying, 'I'm the doctor!' . . . Most of all, though, the patients are either on the road to recovery or trying to hang onto the health they've got. They're more like real world people, you know. It does something to someone when they go into a hospital as a patient."

"Oh, believe me, I know."

"So. You had an aneurysm rupture, and you lived to tell about it."

"Yes. I am that patient."

"Okay." She gazed at the notes on her tablet again. "So, first we do your vitals."

The nurse proceeded to wrap a small device around Elaine's wrist. "You know how to lift your arm and hold it across your chest, right?"

"Yeah."

"How are you feeling? Headaches? Blurred vision? Dizziness? Disorientation?"

"No. No. No. Yes."

"Yes? You're disoriented?"

She chuckled. "Oh yes. Not in my head. We just moved from Dallas to Veil. You can't get any more disoriented than that."

"Oh, I see." She stripped off the Velcro cuff. "Your BP is 124 over 72. Pulse is 68. If you do die, can I have your heart?"

"Well, unfortunately I've already given it to my husband Jim."

"Hmm. So I take it your libido is okay." She turned on her tiny, intense flashlight and shined it in Elaine's eyes alternately. "Have you experienced any medical symptoms?"

She sighed. "I do have weakness on my left side, particularly when I get tired. And I sort of have to tell my left foot to start walking sometimes. Sometimes I still feel a little uncoordinated. It's getting better."

"Yeah." Julie made a keyboard appear on her tablet and began to type. "That's the important thing. After all, you're still recovering from a major bleed."

"I know. I get flustered when unexpected things happen. When I have to make snap decisions. And occasionally I still have my episodes where I zone out for a few seconds. They aren't full seizures. Just little spells where I lose consciousness."

The nurse glanced at her. "You're on driving restrictions, right?"

She nodded. "For six months. Well, six months after I stop having episodes where I blank out."

"Are you still doing your physical and occupational exercises?"

"Faithfully. . . . You know, my biggest problem though?"

She was typing again. "What's that?"

"I can't tell when I'm dreaming."

Her eyebrows arched. She gazed at Elaine. "What do you mean?

"Um. It's like I wake up, but my dreams don't turn off. Before the aneurysm, when I woke up whatever I was dreaming disappeared. Poof. Now—not always, but sometimes—I wake up and I know I'm awake, but my mind keeps dreaming."

"Actually that sounds kind of cool. Never tell that to a neurology resident. He'll want to do research on you and write a paper."

"Well I did tell my doctor in Dallas. She gave me some experimental drug. Either it works pretty good or my episodes are diminishing."

"And I take it these episodes are really upsetting to you?"

"Oh my god. You have no idea what it's like to know you're awake, but not know whether what you're seeing is real or a dream. Like last night."

"Last night?"

"Yeah." She stood up abruptly, surprising both the nurse and herself. "Here, I'll show you."

Elaine walked into the dining room and turned to face the bay windows. She inched along the floor until she was standing precisely where she had been the night before. An expression of casual curiosity on her face, hands in her jacket pockets, Julie stood beside her.

"Right here. I came out of my bedroom to take one of the pills." She glanced at the nurse. "I only take them now when the dreams are bad. And I had left nightlights on all through the house since it was our first night here. Just when I was right here, I thought I saw something outside from the corner of my eye. So I stopped and looked out there."

"And what did you see?"

She sighed. "At first it was just a moving shadow, like the gazebo itself was moving or something. Then I realized it was the shape of a man digging. That's when I said, 'Oh, I must be dreaming,' because yesterday afternoon a workman came and dug all around it. I thought I was dreaming about that. But then the man stepped out from behind the gazebo. He was bent over at first, like he was pulling something. Then he got up completely and just stood there and I recognized his shape. It was our neighbor, Chief Daughtry. I met him yesterday too. He was just standing there looking. I couldn't tell if he was looking at me or if he was staring in the other direction."

"And then—poof—he disappeared?"

"Oh no." She folded her arms across her chest, just as she had the night before. "It dawned on me that if he was looking in this direction instead of looking the other way, then he was staring right at me. I'm sure anyone outside could've seen me with the nightlights. I felt very self-conscious. So I went in the kitchen and took my pill."

"And when you came out, he was gone?"

"Yes. . . . Well, that's his house behind the cedar bushes over there. I thought I saw someone disappear through there."

The nurse pursed her lips. "These dreams-that-don't-turn-off, do they start after you wake up, or do they start before you wake up and then continue on?"

"Oh, they always start when I'm sleeping."

"Well then, what you experienced last night might be your common, garden variety hallucination or something, but it couldn't have been one of your dreams. It didn't start until you were awake and halfway to the kitchen."

Elaine stared at her, reflecting. The possibility that she actually had seen a man at the gazebo in the darkness filled her with astonishment, uncertainty and excitement.

"Can I show you something? It will only take a minute."

Julie glanced at her watch. "I'm all yours, for seventeen minutes and thirty seconds."

She led the nurse through the door from the living room into the backyard.

"So you can see where Antonio dug out around the corners of the foundation yesterday, right?

"Sure."

"What do you notice back here?" She stood at the back of the structure, the corner closest to the Daughtry's yard.

"Well, there's a lot more dug out here. It looks as if they removed some dirt from between the pilings."

"Yeah. That's what I thought. Do you notice anything else?"

"Like what?"

"Do you notice anything about the wood itself?"

"You mean the shovel marks?"

"Exactly." She stepped back to give the nurse room. "Where else do you see them?"

Hands still in the pockets of her jacket, Julie walked around the wooden structure. She came back and gazed at the dimpled redwood, as if to be sure of what she was seeing, and then walked around the gazebo a second time.

"Well . . . I only see them right here."

"Me too. Only where I saw Sheriff Daughtry standing."

Julie arched her eyebrows. "You said you didn't know if he was looking in your direction or in the opposite direction?"

"Yeah."

20

"Well. I mean if he was digging around this, he wouldn't be facing away from your house. You don't turn your back to something and dig under it."

". . . Meaning he did see me."

The nurse stood silently, intently considering. Whether it was the situation or how to respond to it, Elaine wasn't sure. At last she said, "You know what I'm feeling right now?"

"What?"

"Two things. First, I'm feeling an over-abundance of caution. I'd say there's a 95% chance that the contractor's man ran into something right there—an old stump or maybe a trumpet vine—that he had to dig up. I'd say this is completely explainable. Then, too, I suppose that leaves a 5% chance the policeman did come over here. Maybe he knew you were going to do something to the gazebo and he had something buried here that he needed to recover."

"Like what?"

"I don't know. Guns. His stash of retirement money he extorted from drug dealers. How should I know? As far as I'm concerned, I don't want to know. His bullet doesn't have my name on it. . . . On the other hand, I was also going to say it's your yard and you have a perfect right to find out if someone was back here digging around last night and why they were doing it."

Elaine felt herself begin to smile, a slow smile that spread across her face. "So in other words, you're saying I should drop this like a hot potato. And also that I ought to make sure to check it out."

"Exactly."

She nodded. "You've spent a little too much time working around doctors. Want to go inside and have a glass of iced tea?"

"That would be really nice, if I can just use your bathroom first. I also have to finish our initial evaluation and interview."

"Okay." Elaine held the door for her nurse. "So how often are you going to come and check on me?"

"Couple times a week. Unless you stop making progress. Or you find something sinister about your neighbor you're just dying to share with me."

She was in her bedroom staring at the mini-blinds and trying to decide whether it was worth it to get new window treatments when she heard Camille roar again.

21

"Mom! It's a lady!"

Elaine shook her head and walked out of the bedroom and down the hall to the front door. Camille was holding it only part way open as if uncertain about letting the stranger on the porch see inside the house. Elaine pulled the door and her daughter toward her and saw a short, pair-shaped, fiftyish woman with steel gray hair standing on the porch. She was holding a casserole dish covered with aluminum foil.

"Hello," the woman said, smiling pleasantly. "I'm your neighbor, Sheila."

"Oh, come in! Come in!" Elaine stepped out of the doorway, bumping Camille with her hip. "Go tweet your friends, honey."

She led the way down the hall to the living room gazing over her shoulder at her neighbor. "So you're Mrs. Daughtry."

"Yes."

"I'm Elaine Randolph. Let's push aside some boxes and sit in the living room."

"I heard you and your husband both met my man Larry yesterday."

"We did." She sat on the sofa making a spot on the coffee table for Sheila to set down the casserole dish.

"Well let me assure you—" She placed the dish on the table and leaned back against the cushion. "—you are not under investigation. That's just his way."

She laughed. "Well, Chief Daughtry explained that's the treatment all new Veil residents receive."

"I have to admit, we have been so curious about you all ever since we heard you were moving in. There's such a thin line sometimes between being friendly and just being nosy."

"It doesn't bother us at all. We are going to be neighbors and we need to get acquainted. It's hard for us to go knock on doors around here when we're up to our elbows in unopened boxes."

Sheila leaned forward. "Well now seriously, hon, if you need something moved while your husband is at work, you let me know and I'll have Larry come do the grunt work."

"Thank you so much. For most of the heavy stuff I have my son Jake. He doesn't like helping, but I just hide his iPod until he does what I tell him." She crossed her legs. "Speaking of getting acquainted, my little girl Cammie was wondering if there were any children her age around here."

An instantaneous expression of something like distress flashed across the neighbor's face, replaced immediately with a casual smile. "Yes. As a matter of fact there are twin girls, Natalie and Madelyn Short who live just a few houses down. How old is—"

"Cammie is eleven."

"Well I think Nattie and Maddie are right along in there. Ten or eleven. They are great fun. They're identical. I could never tell them apart until Maddie chipped one of her front teeth on the edge. And a couple blocks over are the Halvorson girls. Three of them spread two years apart—thirteen, eleven and nine."

"Wow. That took some planning."

Sheila nodded slyly. "Herb was career Army. Darlene said she got pregnant every time he would come home after a deployment. No need to take birth control while he was gone and they'd get too impatient for sex when he got home."

"I see. Now I believe your husband said you have a daughter too. She lives over in the mid cities?"

"Yes, we do. That's our darling Susan. She lives in Bedford."

"She's a single career girl, I take it?"

"Well she's single. I don't know about the career. I think she'd like to get married one day. So far no one has passed the test."

"The test, huh?" Elaine chuckled. "She's looking for Mr. Right?"

Sheila shook her head. "It's not so much her test. She's trying to find the guy her dad can live with. For some reason he doesn't like her choice in boyfriends."

"Oh. I guess that can be pretty intimidating, dating the police chief's daughter."

"I guess. Personally I'd settle for any red-blooded, gainfully employed male who can produce me some grandchildren."

"Ha! I see."

"I really enjoy talking to you Mrs. Randolph. I hadn't intended to even come in. I know how busy you must be." The neighbor looked around at the paper, boxes and undistributed knick-knacks littering the room. "Seriously, if you want help, just ask and point. I can put stuff away too."

"Um-hmm. And can you decide where to put stuff?"

"Well, that I'd better leave up to you."

Elaine shook her head slowly. "I have such trouble making decisions now. I guess your husband told you?"

"About your brain injury? Yes. He said you sometimes get a little flustered."

"I do. That's true." She gazed at Sheila, deciding. "Can I ask you something? Neighbor-to-neighbor? Girl-to-girl?"

"Well, yes. I suppose."

Elaine lowered her voice so that only Sheila could hear it. "Mrs. Daughtry, I sometimes have hallucinations. It comes with my recovery. I have them less and less. The problem is, sometimes afterward I don't know if I was hallucinating or not."

"Yes?"

"Well . . . last night I had to go to the kitchen in the middle of the night. As I was walking through this room—and I was standing right over there in the dining room—I thought I saw your husband—just his shadow because it was dark—standing out there beside the gazebo with a shovel. Is that possible?"

After a second or two, the neighbor frowned. "A shovel? You didn't see him with a fishing pole, did you?"

"No."

"Well that's a relief!"

They laughed. Elaine felt her anxiety begin to dissipate.

"So when was this last night?"

"Uh. About 2:30, give or take."

Sheila shook her head. "Well you may have seen someone in your backyard, all right, and I don't mind mentioning that possibility to my husband, the cop. He would want to find out if other people around here saw a stranger wandering around. But I'm pretty sure it couldn't have been Larry."

"Oh?"

"The county had him doing surveillance, Mrs. Randolph. They cut back on the number of deputies in Cochran County when the recession hit so bad. Now, when they need extra help, they call in off duty officers from all the municipalities."

"Oh. I see."

"Last night I took the call myself. The county dispatcher called to ask Larry to go over to Hwy. 5 and watch for some blue mini van. Something about laundering drug money."

"Really? Does that happen often?"

"Well the calls come every couple of weeks. It just happened to be a night off for Larry."

Elaine sighed, gazing down at the buff colored carpet. "I feel so foolish now. My mind plays tricks on me sometimes. I just don't know when what I see is real and when it isn't."

"Well if you think someone—"

"No," she interrupted. "Please don't tell your husband. I feel really embarrassed. I'm glad I asked because, well—"

"I understand." She stood up. "It'll just be between us chickens."

Elaine rose, smiling. "Thank you so much. It was serendipity that you came over today."

"Well I have to say that I really came to bring you dessert."

"Oh." She bent down and pulled the aluminum foil off the dish.

"It's called a 'dump cake.' Doesn't look like much, but take my word for it, it's delicious."

Elaine leaned over the still warm, yellow and red dish, inhaling the sweet fruit flavors.

Her voice was conspiratorial. "You know, as long as we're having this girl-to-girl, personal talk, I have some fresh tea in the kitchen. I think you and I should each have a big fat piece of this cake right now to see if it's any good."

Indecision marked her neighbor's face. "Oh, I don't know, hon. I'm supposed to be on this strict diet."

"Oh, didn't I tell you? The tea is sugar free."

Sheila gave a throaty laugh.

The third visitor of the day, the only one she recognized on site, was her realtor, Janet Thomason. She arrived early in the afternoon as Elaine stood in the kitchen putting the juice tumblers and tea glasses into the cupboard.

The instant the silver Buick with the red-white-and-blue placard—"Star of Texas Realty"—on the driver's door pulled into the driveway, she smiled. Mrs. Thomason, thin, short and as always beautifully attired and frowning, got out with her satchel. Elaine went to the front door immediately and opened it, mostly to prevent Camille from screaming another introduction.

"Hello," she said.

"Hello, Elaine. May I come in?"

"Please do."

Janet gazed around at the stacks of boxes, unsorted household goods and disarrayed furniture as they made their way back into the living room. She sat where Sheila Daughtry had been sitting earlier.

"So I see you have everything organized and put away."

Elaine laughed. "I was hoping you came to help with that."

"I—" She flipped up the leather strap and opened the bag. "— brought your copy of all the closing documents. The Blanchard's filled theirs out without a problem yesterday and everything is in order." She produced a thick manila folder.

"Oh look at that!" Elaine clapped her palms together in mock joy. "More paper."

"Mmm. That's right. We kill a couple trees every time we sell a house. The worst of it is that this was a very simple sale. No mortgage insurance. No homeowner warrantee. No contingencies."

"Well, we Randolph's pride ourselves on being simple people."

Janet laughed for the first time. "So, how do you like it here?"

"After twenty-four hours it's just what the doctor ordered: quiet to the point of boredom. The town of Veil has lived up to its reputation for tranquility."

"I know. I knew this was the place for you. Do you think, after a year, you'll change your mind about moving back to Richardson and stay out here in the boonies?"

She shook her head. "Not if I get well. If I continue to get all my mental and physical abilities back—or as much as I can, at least—I'm sure Jim and the kids will want to go home. So next year we could be asking you to sell this house again."

"Well that could work out okay. If you make a few upgrades— like your fence and built in hot tub. You can ask more for it and actually flip it. You could get all your equity and another ten to twelve percent."

"…Well. You can help us when it gets closer."

Janet closed the leather bag and set it beside the sofa. "I do hope that at least you'll enjoy the house and the little town while you're here."

"Oh it's nice here. People are friendly. They're very helpful. We've met a few of the neighbors and they've offered to help out. Like the Daughtry's."

"Ah, the chief and his wife!" Janet exclaimed. "I was attaching the 'sold' plate to the sign in the yard and they rushed out of their house. Wanted to know all about you. I tried to tell them what I could. Hope I didn't say too much."

"Ha! It's hard not to say everything you know when a policeman is doing the asking." Elaine shrugged. "I guess we'll gradually get acquainted with everyone in the neighborhood."

"What about your husband? Is he going to cotton to that long, daily commute?"

She shrugged. "When we lived in California, he had a commute almost that long, but he took the train. Public transportation doesn't really exist in Texas, so we'll see how he does. My hope is that I can make some home cooked meals for him to look forward to. When I was a nurse and working my thirty-six hours every week, we brought in a lot of food and ate out a lot. I guess we'll see if I can still cook. In the meantime, we found out that they do have a good pizza parlor in town."

"Pizza. My son lived on that while he was in college. Well, what about your children? I guess you'll have to wait for school to start before you find out whether they like it here or not."

"My son Jake," she said slowly, "is a smart ass of the first order. He views this year as a sort of 'foreign' exchange' trip to the nation of 'Redneck'. He thinks this is a total hoot. We keep counseling him not to insult people. Him—I think he'll be fine when he meets a few kids and find out they have as much attitude as he does.

"Now, Camille . . . I really feel for her because she was so attached to her little girl friends. Sheila Daughtry put us onto some other girls in this neighborhood. Maybe finding someone her age around here to play with will ease her through the move."

A strange expression crossed Janet's face. It was the second time Elaine had seen that look in one day. Where else? Ah yes, it was the momentary look Sheila Daughtry had given her when Elaine asked if there were children Camille's age in the neighborhood.

Janet looked down. She toyed with the leather strap on her satchel. She seemed to be wrestling with something, something she felt the need to say.

"Elaine. Mrs. Randolph. I have something I want to tell you." She held up her hand as if motioning someone to slow down. "I personally feel the need to tell you this. I want to stress I don't have to tell you this."

". . . Yes?"

". . . When you and Mr. Randolph got interested in this house—interested enough to make an offer, of course I was very glad, since it was my listing. There was something I learned about the people who lived in this house. Something happened to them. I didn't know if it would make a difference to you all or not. I didn't know if I should tell you. I went to our closing lawyer and asked if we were bound to tell you. You know, legally, if something has happened in a house you're buying, like a tragic death or a crime, we're bound to tell you. Technically nothing happened here, so our lawyer said we didn't have to disclose it. It's been on my mind though. I think, if I were you and Jim, I would want to know."

"What happened to them?"

"They lost a child. It was seven or eight years ago."

"Oh my god. I'm so sorry. Was it an accident?"

". . . You don't understand. I'm saying they literally lost her. She disappeared."

"Oh. Oh no. . . . And did they—"

"Never. To this day she has not been found."

"Well, did they have an idea about what happened? Was she abducted?"

"There was a teenage boy who lived here in Veil. He was seventeen or eighteen. The same night Nicole Blanchard disappeared, this boy disappeared. So, people assumed he took her and—harmed her—and never came back."

"Well, was he ever—"

"Nope. Neither one was ever seen again. Really. I don't want to put any interpretation or pass on any unfounded gossip. I just thought, if I were you, I would want to know."

"Well . . . thank you. I think that's awful for the Blanchard's. I can't imagine how you live through something like that. But—why were you bringing up all that legal responsibility business? Why was it such a big deal for us and our buying this house that the Blanchard family had this tragedy happen to them?

The realtor's face darkened. Her voice cracked with anxiety as she spoke. "Because the last time anyone saw Nicole, she was in her bedroom, the room the Blanchard's kept lavender all these years."

Elaine stared at her, trying to apprehend the magnitude of what she had been told. Slowly she said, "You're telling me that a ten-year-old girl was abducted out of the same room my eleven-year-old daughter slept in last night?"

Janet shook her head. "We don't know that. The last anyone saw of her, she was in that bedroom. The next day, she was just gone. She might have gotten out of the house. Who knows?"

"But you are telling me that the child who happened to be almost the same age as my child and who slept in my daughter's bedroom suddenly disappeared. And was never seen again?"

"Yes, I suppose I am."

Elaine sat, staring, for an instant. She felt herself begin to rise. Janet was speaking again. Elaine could hear the words, but the words did not register with her consciousness, just as her own actions were divorced from her intentions. She felt herself stand sluggishly and step in the direction of the lavender room, the room where her baby, her daughter, innocent and dear, was alone and unknowing. This was the same feeling she had when she became overly excited and her mind momentarily shut down to reset itself. She knew what was coming. Before she lost awareness, she heard her voice cry a single word.

"Cammie!"

She was lying on the sofa looking up. Janet, bent at the waist, stood above her, adjusting Elaine's position so she wouldn't slide onto the floor. Camille, curious and slightly concerned, appeared in her field of vision.

"Are you all right, Mom?"

"She just fainted, honey," Janet replied.

"I heard her call for me."

"Yes. I think she felt it coming on. Would you go tell your brother what happened? And tell him she's going to be fine."

"Okay." The child disappeared.

Elaine pushed down with her arms, struggling to get up right. Janet put a hand on each shoulder, lifting her to a sitting position. Elaine took a slow deep breath, trying to gather herself as she had been taught.

"How long?"

"Were you out? Maybe thirty seconds."

". . . A bad one."

"It scared the hell out of me. I guess it was my fault."

"No. No. I'm glad you told me." She looked up at the realtor.

"They couldn't tell if the boy broke into the house and got the girl?"

"This is Veil, Texas, Elaine. Nobody locks their doors or windows."

"Mom?" Jake was standing before her. Camille was behind him, gazing around his shoulder. "Are you all right?"

"I will be, son." She straightened. "Jake. You have to do something for me."

"What?"

"I need you to change rooms with your sister."

"What? No way."

"Right now, son."

"Oh no, Mom. Everything is unpacked. I've almost started putting my clothes away. I already flattened the boxes."

"No shortage of boxes, son. I'll loan you all you need."

"But Mom—" He stepped toward her, his hands outstretched and open. "—her room is purple. Light purple. I'll never be able to bring anybody over here. Dude! Every kid in this town probably knows that's a purple bedroom. No telling what will happen to me. It's like—taking girl hormones or something."

She forced a smile. "I'll call your dad. He'll bring home some black paint. Everything will be all right."

"Why, Mom?"

"Yeah, why?" Camille piped in. "I like that room. It's nice and private."

Elaine sighed. Making sure not to glance at Janet, she replied, "That's just it. It makes me a little nervous to have Cammie off by herself like that. You can take care of yourself, Jake. Now, please, let's make this change. Start now and you can be finished before your dad gets home with supper."

Jake turned immediately. He made a huffing sound as he walked away. "You need to get well, Mom, before I'm stunted for life."

"Hey, Mom. When you call Dad, can I also have some paint for my new room? A nice yellow?"

"I'll pass that on, my love."

Cammie skipped as she left, totally unconcerned. The two women were left alone in the suddenly quiet living room. Janet gazed down at her client.

"Are you okay now, Elaine?"

"Yes. I'm going to be all right."

"Well." She sighed. She bent down and picked up her bag. "I guess I've brought all the joy and sunshine I can for one day. I think I need to get out of here."

"Janet."

The realtor looked back at Elaine, sitting on the couch, still trying to restore mental and emotional order.

"I'm glad you told me. I know you didn't have to. Thank you for telling me."

Janet considered her words. "I don't know whether to say 'you're welcome' or 'I'm sorry'."

"Is there anything else you can tell me about the kidnapping?"

She sighed. "I remember when it happened. This whole part of the state was upset. All kinds of police officers and investigators were crawling all over the place. I never could understand why they couldn't find the little girl."

Elaine tilted her weary, wobbly head. "What I can't understand is why all these neighbors we've been meeting haven't said a word about this."

"They probably think you know all about it. That you'll bring it up if you want to discuss it. I just know I couldn't go on any longer without telling you. A guilty conscience drives me crazy." She shrugged. "Maybe that's why I don't sell anymore houses than I do."

# Chapter 3

She had not been sitting at the kitchen table long enough to finish her half glass of mineral water when Jim appeared. He pulled out a chair adjacent to her.

"Is this a private insomnia session, or can anybody brood?"

She smiled. "I'm sorry. I sure didn't mean to wake you up and, really, I didn't think I had."

"It's something about you just not being beside me. All that time you spent in the hospital and in rehab, I never did get used to you not being there. And when I sense you aren't there . . . I don't know. I guess, when it comes to you, I've become very vigilant."

"I'm sorry. I know the whole reason we came here was so all of us could just back down from our shared high anxiety."

Jim shook his head. "Two nights in our new boring place and no serenity for you yet. We may as well have stayed in Richardson."

Nodding, she said, "I bet that's what you think when you're making that long drive every day."

"Oh it's not so bad. Darren McCoy—remember him—once got a temporary assignment to Garden City, Kansas. He had to be there for eighteen months. So he took a calendar and wrote how many days were left. Each day he put an 'x' and said out loud, 'I just got 425 more days.'"

She studied his sleepy face. "You and Jake. Never miss a chance to tell me in subtle ways how I've disrupted your lives."

"Really." He arched his eyebrows. "I thought I was consoling you for making my life a living hell." After they laughed, he asked, "So, are you sitting here thinking about the little girl?"

"No, actually, I went to sleep thinking about her, but fifteen or twenty minutes ago I woke up and thought I heard someone in the house. So I got up and crept around. I was trying to be quiet."

"So the burglar could work in peace?"

"No, because I always proceed from the notion these days that whatever is bothering me or whatever I heard or saw is mostly just in my head. So I checked on the kids. I checked all the doors and windows. Nothing."

"Well—" He yawned. "—from what I've heard about this little town, a burglary would be front page news."

"Yes. I expect it would. Can you imagine what it was like when the little girl disappeared? It must've been horrendous. Beyond belief. . . . Which makes me wonder, if something unforgettable like that happens in a house, or might have happened, and you buy that house a few years later, why don't the neighbors come tell you about it? I mean, I understand Janet's dilemma. She was playing by the rules. She didn't have to say anything before the sale. Then afterwards she just felt like she needed to. But why hasn't anyone else mentioned it?"

Jim leaned forward, setting his elbows on the table. "I don't think that's so mysterious. I'm guessing they all assume we already know about it. I think it's one of those big unspoken topics that every family or little community has and everyone knows not to bring it up. The elephant in the room that nobody mentions. The neighbors probably just discuss it in private."

Elaine gazed past him, down the dark hallway.

"Hello? Did I lose you dear?"

"You just gave me a thought. Since this was such a big deal here in Veil, I bet the local paper wrote all kinds of stories about it."

"Well there is no local paper."

"There isn't?"

"Nope. Local news around here is covered by the daily county paper, the Cochran Sentinel."

"So should I go over there in the morning?"

Jim frowned. "That's sort of a long walk isn't it, to Cochran?"

"Oh. How—"

"Fifteen miles. And I'm not sure little newspapers keep searchable archives like that."

"Somebody had to keep a record of it."

"Well, if you'll let me finish. If I don't miss my guess, either the local library or the one over in Cochran will have those on microfiche. Call and find out and if you still want to read up on it, I'll try to come home early one night when the library's open and take you over there."

"Okay. If you don't mind."

"As for me—" He stretched and stood. "—I have to get up in

four hours and get ready for work. I do have one more question for you, though."

"Yes?"

"What do you hope to gain by reading about this missing child?"

Elaine sighed. She rolled her water glass back and forth between her hands.

"Honestly, I don't know. Maybe, when I read the circumstances, I'll be less spooked." She looked up at him. "You should be grateful, though."

"Why is that?"

"Because at least it's taken my mind off seeing our neighbor digging in our backyard last night."

His face assumed the big, sly grin she found so attractive when they first met—the grin he had handed down to Jake. "What if they're connected?"

"What?"

"Yeah. What if it was the little girl's body the chief was digging out from under our gazebo."

"Oh my god, Jim! What an awful thing to say. Go to bed. From now on I'll brood by myself, if you don't mind."

After Elaine finished her phone call, she sat quietly on the living room sofa considering her options. The most mature, wisest thing to do—the grown up inside her said—was to wait until Jim could come home early one day and drive her over to Cochran. Something else in her—something impetuous, adventurous, prophetic—told her not to wait.

She got up and walked down the hall to Jake's new bedroom. At first she was going to knock on the door, but realized he wouldn't hear her anyway. So she turned the handle carefully. He was standing near the far wall, slapping taupe paint on it with a long handled roller.

When he realized she had come into the room, he lowered the roller and pulled out his ear buds.

Hands on hips, she surveyed the sea of plastic drop cloths punctuated abundantly with brown. "Getting any paint on the walls there, son?"

He shook his head. "I got to tell you, Mom, this crazy purple is hard to cover. Going to take two coats at least."

"So, Jake, I wonder if you'd be willing to take a break and do me another favor."

He set the business end of the roller on the drop cloth. "I am not painting Cammie's new room. If she wants to go off and play with her new little friends, that's cool. But I don't have to pick up the slack for her."

"Jake, as I look at your work here it occurs to me that you are the least likely person in the universe I would ask to paint another room in this house. No, what I was hoping was that you would drive me somewhere."

His jaw dropped. "Drive? As in car keys and turn signals and all?"

"Yep."

"Well that's cool. Is it legal? I mean, I only have a learner's permit and you are under doctor's order not to drive."

"Hey," she said confidently. "You have a permit and I am a licensed driver, well over the necessary age limit to sit in the passenger's front seat. We're 100% legal."

"Cool freaking beans." He frowned. "So is this 'drive six blocks to the grocery store for things you need for supper'?"

"No. This is 'drive to the county public library over in Cochran'."

He paused. "That's like . . ."

"Fifteen miles. Each way."

"Oh my god. An actual drive." His eyes narrowed. "What's Dad going to think about this?"

"Are you planning to tell your father about it?"

"No."

"I'm sure not going to say anything to him about it."

"Oh my god." He danced in place and ratcheted his arms as if playing an electric guitar. "Outlaw Mom!"

"Get your permit while I get my purse."

He stood still and solemnly pulled a billfold from the back pocket of his jeans. "I have it here. I always keep it right with me. You know, just in case."

"Right. Let me lock the doors and get my purse."

"I'll be in the driver's seat."

She checked the exterior doors and made sure the coffee maker was turned off.

It was 10 a.m. Thirty minutes over to Cochran. Thirty minutes back. An hour to look at files. They should be back in time for lunch with no problem. If Jim called and didn't get them, he'd assume Jake was listening to music and that Cammie and she were outside.

Jake was indeed sitting in her Nissan with the engine running and the garage door open. He was wearing sunglasses and staring straight ahead with a fearsome expression, like a warrior awaiting the commencement of dubious battle. Elaine did her best not to laugh as she slid into the passenger's seat and closed her door.

"All right, son," she said. "This car is my pride and joy. It doesn't have a scratch on it. And we're going to keep it that way."

"Roger that."

She shook her head. "Do you know where those twins live, the Short sisters?"

"Yeah, I think. That dark red brick and light brown roof?"

"Right. Let's go by there and see if we need to take your sister with us."

For all his braggadocio, Jake drove the car quite cautiously. He kept his hand glued to the steering wheel at the "ten-and-two" position and looked three times approaching each intersection. He eased gradually to a stop before the twin's house.

"Allow me," Elaine said, opening her door.

Veronica Short, a beautiful young woman with a mischievous smile, opened the door. Elaine introduced herself and as the two stood getting acquainted, the sisters Madelyn and Natalie appeared, with Camille trailing behind them.

"So why I came over Veronica, was to say that my son Jake is driving me over to Cochran on an errand. We'll be gone maybe two hours and be back around lunchtime. I came to see if I needed to take Cammie with us."

Mrs. Short glanced back at her daughters, who said in unison, "Can she stay, Mom? Please? Can she?"

"They seem to be having a good time. We don't have any other plans and Camille is welcome to stay unless she'd rather go with you."

"Ride with my brother? I'd much rather stay here than die in a flaming car crash."

The mothers looked at each other.

"You can feel the love, can't you?" Elaine said. "We'll be back by lunch time."

"Take all the time you need. I'll let the girls fix sandwiches around noon."

"The trick will be getting them to clean up."

"They think that's what moms are for. Enjoy yourself and I'll try to think of somewhere I need to go without the twins—next week, maybe, when you're all unpacked."

"It's a deal."

Veronica closed the door.

Elaine smiled as she walked back to the car, thinking what a lovely, pleasant, hospitable person Veronica Short was, and making a mental note never to introduce her to Jim.

"All right, chauffer. I got directions so let's go."

Because of the timing of her surgery and the length of her recuperation, she had never ridden while Jake drove. She watched him from the corner of her eyes, determined to say as little as possible, and trying not to smile. She gave him turning directions well in advance and he followed them wordlessly.

The Cochran County Government Center—including the post office, county courthouse and library—formed a "U" in front of a common parking lot. Jake crept along the rows of vehicles looking for an empty space.

"I don't mind the walk. Really."

"Okay."

He jumped at the chance to move to the end of the lot closest to the street and furthest from the buildings. There he found ample parking, with no need to maneuver between parked cars. He pulled into a space, put the car in park and shut the engine off and sighed.

Elaine smiled broadly. "I thank you and my Nissan thanks you."

"So what am I supposed to do? Sit here and wait?"

She opened her door. "I anticipate it may be a little less than an hour, which is a really long time to sit in a car in Texas in the summer. There is the courthouse and I'm sure there is a jail in there somewhere if you want to visit your friends. There's the Post Office in case you have something to mail—oh wait, you're part of the digital generation, aren't you? You don't believe in snail mail. Behind door number three is the library, where you can come in and stay cool, read books and magazines, get a library card and—oh yes—also surf the internet. The choice is yours."

"Okay." He opened his door and stepped out. I'm coming with you. Shall I keep the keys?"

"Yes, dear."

There were a number of differences she observed, between this relatively new library and the California libraries she had used when she was a child. In contrast to the stone steps leading up to a main floor, this library was barrier free. Rather than a desk at the front giving way to a forest of stacks behind it, this library was spacious, with a high ceiling and colorful reading areas visible in the different sections and with the checkout desk in the center of the room. And, as opposed to a frowning, matronly librarian, there was a security guard sitting beside electronic sensors in the shape of a doorframe.

"I'm going to the computers," Jake murmured and immediately disappeared.

Elaine found her way to the desk marked "Reference Librarian."

The young man behind it was standing and watching a monitor as he maneuvered a computer mouse.

"Excuse me. My name is Elaine Randolph. I—"

"Oh, Mrs. Randolph. I'm Eric. We talked just a few minutes ago." He came around the desk and motioned toward a bank of machines sitting inconspicuously against the wall. "I was not here seven years ago when that event transpired and I had not heard about it. So I was curious myself. Managed to do a little research."

He pulled out a chair for her in front of one of the machines. As he spoke, he loaded film into the machine and rapidly moved the viewfinder to the particular day he wanted.

"Now the Sentinel published front page stories on the child for the first week after she disappeared. I didn't have the chance to search for later articles."

"This is way more than I expected," she said. "I can't tell you how much I appreciate it."

"Well that's my job. I hope you find all you're looking for. And if you want copies of any screen—see this button here? Push it and a photocopy will be printed over there by the checkout counter. It's fifteen cents a copy."

"Thank you so much."

"Just let me know if you need anything else." He hurried away from her as quickly as he had hurriedly brought her to the machine.

She took a breath and looked at the first screen, the image of a Sunday edition of the Cochran Sentinel. A bold double headline proclaimed: "Manhunt Underway For Missing Veil Girl." There was a black and white photograph of a sweet-faced, guileless child, captioned "Nicole Blanchard." She pushed the button to make a copy of the page and then read the article.

*Police, Cochran County Deputies and the Texas Highway Patrol have joined the search for missing Nicole Blanchard, ten-year-old daughter of Clay and Valerie Blanchard of Veil.*

The child was reported missing from her bedroom Saturday morning. Police investigators suspect an abduction in the case. Because there were no signs of forced entry into the house, it has been theorized the girl knew her kidnapper.

*The parents of the girl voluntarily submitted to polygraph tests to eliminate themselves as suspects in the abduction.*

The article continued with a discussion of locations where the search was taking place, the response of neighbors and a prayer vigil begun by the Blanchard's church. It concluded with a request for anyone with pertinent information to come forward. It did not, Elaine noted, make any specific mention of any teenage boy who was suspected of being involved.

It took Elaine as long to find the next day's file on the film as it had taken the librarian to load, locate and explain the reader's use. When she did, she saw a photo of the backyard of the house into which her family had just moved.

She studied it in fascination. It was a much larger picture than the snapshot of Nicole that had run the previous day. A uniformed officer was holding a long, leather lead, at the other end of which was a German Shepherd sniffing the row of cedar trees between her backyard and the Daughtry's. The photo had been taken from a distance, so she could see the entire backyard, which was dominated by a sturdy, large, wooden swing set and elevated playhouse. The caption of the photo read, "Troopers use cadaver dogs in search for missing girl."

Elaine sighed and sat back. A feeling of release and relief spread through her in a wave. And in its wake came understanding and sadness.

Whatever Larry Daughtry might have dug up from under the gazebo, if anything, at least it wasn't the bones of Nicole Blanchard.

The gazebo had not been in the backyard when she died. And if the child had been buried in that location, perhaps under the playhouse, the police dogs would have found her. Elaine also grasped the reason the gazebo was built in the first place: the Blanchard's couldn't bear to see the playhouse every day, a nagging reminder of their missing child. The gazebo had been built to replace it. She felt so sorry for them.

The accompanying story had no real news about the investigation and search. It rehashed the reports of the previous day and had nebulous comments from the police and neighbors. It dawned on Elaine as she read the article that Larry Daughtry had not been the Chief of Police then. Another officer was mentioned several times as the chief. Daughtry's name did not appear anywhere in the article.

She found the image of the front page of the Tuesday Sentinel much more quickly. And when she did, she was greeted by a stark, surly photo of an adolescent boy. His expression was so rebellious and sullen she immediately took it for a police photo. It was only after a few seconds of studying it that she realized, like Nicole's photo, it was a school snapshot. His probably came from a high school yearbook.

The lyrics to an old Bruce Springsteen song about the posturing of young adults came to her: "Girls comb their hair in rearview mirrors, and the boys try to look so hard." Elaine smiled. This boy wanted the world to be intimidated by him.

"Teen Sought in Connection With Disappearance of Child," read the bold headlines.

Authorities have widened the scope of their search for missing ten-year-old Nicole Blanchard as they also seek the whereabouts of seventeen-year-old Avery Maxwell. Maxwell, a junior at Veil High School, has not been seen since late Friday night, the time around which the Blanchard child disappeared. Maxwell was known to have been in the area on the evening in question.

For the third time, Elaine pushed the button to make a copy of an article. She rolled the words of the newspaper story around in her thoughts.

"What does that mean," she murmured, "'known to have been in the area?'" She assumed the Maxwell boy must not have lived in the neighborhood, else why would they point out he had been in the *vicinity. How did they know he had been around there?*

The article had a description of his car, "an older four-door Mitsubishi compact, dark-blue, with Texas plates XXC-1421." Again, readers with information were asked to contact the police.

By the time she pulled up the seventh image of the Sentinel's front page, Elaine was much quicker at running the scanner. She read the article that had appeared in the paper that Saturday with resignation and sadness.

How difficult it must've been for the Blanchards. Only a week had passed since their daughter disappeared, but it must've seemed like months. And, now, seven years later, Elaine was reading their heartbreaking story and knowing how it ended. Or rather, that it didn't end. That the child was not found, neither dead nor alive. That the boy who took her was never apprehended.

She tilted her head from side to side, looking at the last page. By the seventh day the event was already losing its prominence. It was no longer at the top of the front page, but in a corner at the bottom with a headline smaller and not nearly so bold. Just like that, the significance of a child's life ebbed away. That, too, must've increased the helpless dismay of the girl's parents.

How, Elaine wondered, did a seventeen-year-old boy kidnap a child and disappear from the face of the earth? Police all over Texas and all over Oklahoma, Arkansas and Louisiana must've been watching for the old, dark-blue Mitsubishi. It would have been one thing to take the girl and run, to evade detection for a day or two or three, but how could a teenager find the resources—the money, the clothes, the shelter—to keep from being discovered? Even if he had quickly killed the girl and disposed of her body, there were limits to the capabilities of an adolescent, not even eighteen. Had someone helped him? It was difficult for Elaine to conceive of Avery Maxwell abducting Nicole Blanchard; even more difficult to imagine neither of them had ever been seen again.

She turned off her reader, removed the file and slid it back into the paper cover. The librarian, she found, was sitting at his reference desk consumed in another project.

"Where do I refile this?" she asked softly.

"Oh, Mrs. Randolph." He stood. "I'll be glad to take it. Did you find what you were looking for?"

"Yes, I did. It put to rest some questions I had. Unfortunately it just created some others." She nodded toward the checkout desk. "I pick up my copies over there?"

"Yes ma'am. You let me know if I can help in the future."

"I will. I will. Thank you so much."

Elaine retrieved her copies and rolled them into the shape of a tube and stuck them into her purse in such a way that they protruded several inches from it. She strolled through the spacious room to the computer camels, where she found Jake playing an on-line video game she had never seen.

"You ready, driver?"

"Wait, wait, wait." He muttered.

There was the muted sound of an explosion from the computer and the monitor showed a flash of yellow, orange and red.

"Who's the king now?" He closed the internet application and stood up. "Where to, boss?"

"Just home. Safe and sound. If you drive safely, I'll get us lunch at that hamburger place in Veil."

They walked through the scanner at the front of the library and into the bright, late morning sunshine. Jake pulled her key ring from his pocket.

"I need to get my own set of keys," he said. "One without all this lady stuff."

"Lady stuff?"

"You know, jangly things. Grocery discount cards. I need one with just the keys to your car. And Dad's car."

She smiled. "Right. I'm sure your father will go for that."

As they approached her Nissan, Jake pointed the remote and pushed a button. The door latches popped up.

"Well, hi, neighbor!"

It was a man's voice, familiar and yet intensely distasteful. She looked in the direction of the sound. Chief Larry Daughtry walked toward them.

"Oh. Oh, hello, Chief."

"Larry. Just call me Larry."

"What are you . . ." She stared at him.

"What am I doing here? Well, I'm headed over to the courthouse to pick up some legal documents." He stopped beside Jake, close enough that he could look almost directly down on him. "Well you must be Jacob James Randolph. How are you, son?"

Jake gazed at him without speaking.

Turning his focus back to Elaine, Daughtry smiled disarmingly. "So what are you all doing here?"

"Getting library cards." She responded quickly.

"Just for two of you?"

"Dad doesn't have time to read," Jake replied. "And my sister is illiterate."

"Jake, please. No, Cammie wanted to stay and play with her new friends."

Daughtry nodded. "Short girls, I'll bet. Twins are fun, aren't they? Sheila says she's never sure which one she's talking to." He eyed the rolled photocopies jutting from Elaine's purse. "Well, I guess I'd better get in the courthouse. Got to serve some warrants. Keep all you law-abiding citizens safe. Jacob, you drive safe."

"Yeah, I will."

"Bye now." He turned his back and walked through the rows of parked vehicles toward the courthouse.

Elaine got into the car without speaking. Jake buckled his seatbelt and turned on the engine. He rolled down the window, waiting for the interior of the car to cool.

"That was weird, Mom. That guy just showing up here."

She nodded. "Small world isn't it?"

"I can understand him coming to the courthouse from the Veil cop shop, but how did he happen to park out here where we ended up. All the policemen park over there. See?"

She gazed toward the courthouse, where a dozen or more different marked cars sat in close proximity. Indeed there was a sign designating an area especially for them: "Authorized Vehicles Only." Just one row over from her Nissan was Larry Daughtry's police car.

"Do you suppose he just happened to follow us over here?" she asked.

"And waited in his car for thirty minutes for us to come out? No, Mom, I would have seen him if he had followed us. We drove right by the police station when we left town and his car was there. And I didn't see it all the way over here. He was never behind us."

She chuckled. "Really? And how do you know that?"

He turned to her as if she were missing something obvious. "He has the only Hemi in town."

"What?"

"See his car? It's a Charger with a Hemi engine. All the other police cars that I've seen in Veil are Fords. Crown Vic's. . . . It's like he knew we were coming here."

Elaine silently considered his words. "How did he know your full name?"

Jake shook his head. "It's like he saw it on my learner's permit or something."

# Chapter 4

Elaine stood at the kitchen window, hands on hips, watching as Julie Johnson pulled into the driveway at 8 a.m. She opened the front door and the approaching nurse came to a stop, a wary expression on her face.

"Is this really good or really bad?"

"This is 'I really need someone I can talk to right now.'"

"You know I don't do marriage counseling."

"That comes later. Come in. You want some coffee?"

"Am I going to need some?"

"Actually yes. I have some made."

They sat at the kitchen table until finally, without looking up from her cup, Elaine spoke.

"I had a little adventure yesterday."

"Like a health adventure? One of your little spells at an inopportune moment?"

"No. Like a trip over to the library in Cochran."

The nurse's eyes grew wide in alarm. "You drove to Cochran?"

"Simmer down. I rode with my sixteen-year-old son. For the first time. That's not even the adventure."

"All right." Her voice was cautious.

Elaine turned the spoon round and round in the black liquid. "I found out after you were here the other day that a child was abducted from this house. It was a little more than seven years ago. She was ten."

"I remember that. Someone took her out of her bedroom. A teenage kid kidnapped her, it seems like. And they never found either one. . . . That was this house?"

"Yes. The little girl was Nicole Blanchard. When I heard the story and found out she was kidnapped from the same room my daughter was sleeping in, I have to admit I did freak out a little."

"I sure would have. So how did that become an adventure?"

"I got really curious about it. I couldn't understand why none of the neighbors ever said anything about it. So I talked Jake into driving me to the library. The reference guy over there helped me look up the original newspaper stories."

"Yes?"

"It was really very sad. I can't imagine what the girl's parents must have gone through. And I saw a picture of the boy—Avery Maxwell—they suspected of taking her."

Julie nodded. "So that was your adventure?"

"No."

"Oh. Okay. You know you're giving me the jitters here."

"Sorry." Elaine drew a deep breath. "You remember my neighbor, the police chief, Mr. Daughtry?"

"The one who digs around your gazebo in the middle of the night?"

"Yes. Well, when I found out about this little girl's disappearance, I pretty much stopped thinking about him. That business with the shovel in the backyard suddenly wasn't at the top of my list of concerns. But yesterday, as Jake and I were coming out of the library, who do we find parked next to us but Larry Daughtry."

"Small world."

"Not that small. He had to have followed us to the library."

Julie's face wrinkled. "The library is next to the county courthouse. He probably—"

"Yes that's what he said. Only all the police and sheriff's cars were parked over by the courthouse. Jake and I parked way out in the boonies. He intentionally parked right beside us and he picked the perfect moment when we came out of the library to suddenly appear and speak to us. It was like he came out of nowhere. He starts asking us all these intrusive questions, like it was his business." She studied Julie's skeptical reaction and continued. "Now I'm not the only one who found that peculiar. My son, 'Mr. Oblivious', was the one who pointed out how strange this was. It's like the chief is keeping tabs on us."

Julie sighed. "So, assuming he is—and I'll concede the guy may have done some strange things since you've been here—what's his purpose? Why would he follow you?"

"Beats me." Elaine shrugged. "Maybe his wife told him that I asked about the backyard deal and he's trying to intimidate me into dropping it."

"You aren't thinking his behavior has anything to do with the missing girl, are you?"

"No. How could it? As far as he knows, we never even heard of Nicole. I just want the guy to leave me alone and stop creeping us all out. I wonder if the guy is a stalker. And if he is, who would I call about that? Can you call the police to report the police chief?"

"You think it's a physical thing? Like he's obsessed with you?"

"That would be extremely hard to believe. What kind of a sicko is drawn to an invalid who passes out every time she gets excited?"

"This is Texas. Don't underestimate our perverts."

"Anyway, I don't think there's anything special about me. His wife told me he treats everyone with the same obnoxious scrutiny. I think he just wants to spook new people a little and let them know who's the boss. His way of telling 'em to mind their own business." She blew across the top of her cup and took a sip. "I'm really glad you're willing to talk to me about this. Even if it's all just in my head. I mean, now that I've snuck around and got Jake to drive me without Jim knowing about it, I can't take my husband into my confidence."

"Having Jake drive you to Cochran is not a hanging offense. It may be illegal." She tipped her head to one side. "But it's nothing your husband is going to leave you over."

"Well that's just it. I'm not through being an outlaw. Today I'm going to have Jake take me on another trip. Is it a hanging offense if he drives me to Mt. Pillow?"

"Mt. Pillow? That's probably thirty miles. Why would you go there?"

"To introduce myself to Valerie and Clay Blanchard."

"Blanchard? The parents of the little girl?"

"And the people we bought this house from. Actually we never met them. It was a double closing."

"Just out of curiosity, what do you hope to gain from meeting them?"

Elaine gazed down. "To tell them I'm sorry about their daughter. To tell them we'll let them know if we ever hear anything about Nicole. . . . To ask if Nicole's disappearance is the reason they sold their house and moved away."

"Chances are they moved because of his job. Or even hers."

She shook her head with an ironic smile. "Clay Blanchard is a forensic accountant. He can work anywhere there's an internet connection. Valerie is a teacher. She taught middle school special ed right up until they moved at the end of the last school year."

"You know . . ." Julie began slowly.

"That I'm taking a lot of unnecessary risks? That I'm being nosy? That nothing more than satisfying my curiosity can possibly come out of this?"

"Honestly I was going to say that, for a person who came to Veil to rest, you certainly keep stirring things up."

"Yeah," she sighed, "maybe so. But all this business is interfering with my serenity. I'm still trying to get a good night's sleep."

Julie smiled. "Well, as long as you're talking to the old owners, you might as well kill two birds with one stone and ask if the police chief used to snoop around their backyard at night or turn up unexpectedly when they were out of town."

"I know I'm being paranoid. I know it's all in my head, but that man does creep me out. It's like he knew somehow that Jake and I would be there."

The two women stared at one another.

"You don't suppose that's actually possible, do you?" Elaine asked softly.

"Do you still have the copies of the consent documents I gave you the other day?"

"Sure."

"Well my cell phone number is on them. Take it with you. You can call me any time. You can even text me at that number."

"Thanks." Elaine drew a deep breath. "For some reason that gives me a feeling of peace of mind."

"Yes," Julie said, blowing across her cup. "All a service of your home health nurse."

Julie had only been gone ten minutes when Tim Starling and his crew rolled up. Tim parked his spotless, silver SUV alongside the curb. Behind him was an old, extended cab pickup pulling a long trailer loaded with lots of equipment Elaine had never seen. Half a dozen workers spilled from the truck and began pulling tools off the truck and trailer.

Elaine refreshed her coffee and walked out the living room door to the backyard. The only worker she recognized was Antonio, who interrupted the orders he was giving to his crew to offer her a half salute. She smiled, free hand on her hip as she watched the men swiftly move around the gazebo, preparing to elevate and move it.

"Hello, Mrs. Randolph," Tim said. He stood beside her, his arms folded as he watched the work. "Took us a little longer to get here today than I anticipated. . . . This morning we'll get the standards for the gazebo's new location poured and set. While we're at it, we'll set the foundation for the hot tub. That means we'll move the gazebo to the side and set it on the ground. That won't do it any structural harm, just sitting like that for a few days until we secure it to the new little slab."

"Should I tell my kids to stay out of it?"

"Oh. . . . I suppose so, if six or eight little children got to rocking it, it would tip over. That's the only possible problem—What? . . . Excuse me for a minute, Mrs. Randolph."

One of the workers had called out a question. Elaine didn't hear it, but Starling did and gave the man his immediate, full attention. He left her side and walked to a cluster of workers gathered at the far side of the gazebo, looking down at the dirt. It came to her suddenly that they were standing at the spot where she thought she had seen Larry Daughtry digging.

"Is something wrong, Mr. Starling?" she called.

He glanced over at her. "Wrong? No, ma'am. Just checking out the soil."

She stepped out from under the eaves and walked toward the men. They were looking at the very corner where she thought she had seen a shadowy figure with a shovel. A tall young man was turning earth, drawing it toward himself with a small shovel that had a long, thin blade.

"What did you find?" she asked as casually as possible.

"Sand," Antonio replied.

"Sand?"

"Well, here's the thing," Tim said. "I grew up calling this black dirt 'gumbo,' because it's very waxy and clingy with a high concentration of clay. The saying is, once you stick the blade of a shovel in it, you'll never get all the dirt off again. Only right here under this edge of the gazebo, for some reason, you got a patch of sand."

"Sand," she repeated slowly. "Where'd that come from?"

"Well, Danny here was concerned that it was some kind of

breakdown of the gazebo's foundation. Maybe some kind of rot. But it isn't. I can't think of a way this would be naturally occurring in any soil I know in this area."

"Really?"

"It's like somebody dug a hole here, dumped sand in it and covered it over with topsoil."

What would her therapist tell her to do now, she asked herself. Focus on the coffee mug in her hand. Take deep breaths and blow slowly across it until her heart steadied and her anxiety diminished. Still she couldn't keep herself from asking another question.

"I guess Antonio noticed it Monday afternoon when he checked out the foundation?"

The foreman shook his head.

"Can I ask another question?" she asked. "And I'm not being critical. Just curious. I don't have any complaints."

"You can ask anything you want," Starling responded.

"Well look at the bottom of this redwood." She touched the base of the gazebo with her toe. "See those marks? Are those from Antonio's shovel?"

The foreman stooped, looking closely at the marred wooden beam. "No, no, no," he protested. "I dug toward the foundation. You only get wallowing like that when you dig away from the beam and push your shovel against it."

She nodded. "You know, I absolutely believe you, Antonio. This is the only place where I found those marks. Not in any of the other corners where you dug around the foundation." She looked at Tim. "Isn't that interesting, the one place you find sand instead of 'gumbo' is the one place where someone dug away from the gazebo instead of toward it. What do you make of that?"

Starling shrugged. "Kids is the only thing I can think of. Maybe some youngsters saw us digging around the beam the other day and decided they'd try it as well." He shook his head. "I don't know why they would dig out dirt and dump sand in its place though."

"Makes you wonder. I promise you, though, nobody in my family did this." She took a sip of coffee. "I got to thinking about our conversation the other day. Did you say that Chief Daughtry helped you build this gazebo?"

"Ah. Got in the way mostly is what he did. He had to make a comment on everything we did. All in all, he didn't do much but help us carry lumber. He did help put in the shrubbery though. Said that was the least he could do for the Blanchard's."

"He does like to be helpful. Well, Mr. Starling—Tim, this afternoon my son and I are taking a little drive. Is there anything you need me to do for your crew? You want me to leave the house unlocked? Make some lemonade or tea?"

"Oh no. I wouldn't be comfortable with you doing that, Mrs. Randolph. Y'all are still unpacking from your move and it's a rare move where something doesn't come up missing. I just don't want you and your husband wondering about missing things when my boys have been in your place. We have water on the truck and I have another project not far from here with a portable toilet when they need it."

"Just say the word if you need anything."

He nodded. "I think you're going to be real happy with our work."

"Yes. I know I will. You and your crew have been very helpful."

Mt. Pillow was nothing like Veil. It seemed a much older community, the streets narrower and lined with elms and oaks that provided actual shade. And the terrain was much hillier, the result of limestone substrata scored by an ancient riverbed that had channeled into a small, lovely natural lake. It was a sort of oasis, Elaine thought, from the typical rolling, prairie land of northern Texas, and from the garish bustle of modern life.

"Why is it we didn't think about moving here?" she wondered aloud.

"Because it would have added another half hour to Dad's commute," Jake answered. "And there's no real highway in or out of here."

"I can see why the Blanchard's wanted to move here. You see that intersection ahead? Turn left there."

Elaine had plugged an earpiece into her smart phone to watch the screen and listen to the directions, which she relayed to Jake. She had decided that not hearing the voice of the GPS would be less confusing and stressful for him. She could perceive his confidence behind the steering wheel increasing mile by mile.

"Boy, it didn't take long for Cammie to make new friends, did it?"

"And after you turn, you'll come to an intersection with a traffic signal. Turn left there. . . . No, it didn't. Making friends is a gift of hers."

"Those twins jumped at the chance to have her spend the day with them again."

"The way you jumped at the chance for another long drive through the country? Right at the next intersection."

"Talking nonstop is one of her talents too. You know what they talk about?"

"I can't imagine."

"Me. Didn't you see the way those girls came out to the car and eyeballed me when we pulled up in front of their house. There's no telling what that little snot is saying about me."

"Well, son, as long as you're going to parade through the house wearing just your boxers and playing air guitar, you have to know your sister is going to tell her friends about it." She glanced at his wide-eyed expression. "And the older your sister gets, the older her friends will be. . . . Almost there. Turn right here and drive down this street slow. We're looking for 145."

"Tell me again, why are we coming to see these people?"

"'These people are the Blanchard's. We bought their home, but we never met them. I thought it would be nice to introduce myself. And I have a few things to ask them about the house."

"Like what?"

She pursed her lips. "Like what to do with that sack of money we found in the attic." She smiled when his head snapped toward her.

"Geez, Mom, for a moment I thought you were serious. You got me."

"Well, I have to stay on my toes to keep up with you. Oh, looks like we're in luck."

She motioned toward a driveway and Jake stopped in front of a wood frame cottage, somewhat smaller than the house in Veil, but pretty and quaint with a little porch behind a white wooden railing. Two cars were parked on the end of the drive nearest the side-entry garage. From where they sat in the Nissan, they could see a small dock behind the backyard, and beyond that a still, verdant lake.

"How cool is that? Man, you can walk right out of your house and down to the water."

". . . It's beautiful . . . isn't it?" she replied.

When her speech slowed, Jake turned toward her and studied her face carefully. She focused on the front door of the house, trying to breathe deeply, deliberately.

"Mom? Are you all right? Do we need to go home."

"No. I think I'm okay, Jake. . . . Whew." She sighed.

"You sure you're all right?"

"Tell you what, son. If I pass out, fall over and wet myself, that will be a sign to you that it's time to go home."

He shook his head, his expression mingled relief and disgust. "Nobody has a mom as funny and special as mine."

"Come on, driver."

They got out of the Nissan and walked up the driveway and onto the porch. The sound of the doorbell gave her a momentary feeling of uncertainty. The introduction and plausible excuse she had prepared suddenly seemed preposterous. What would she say? How would she explain their presence?

A heavy set, pleasant-faced man in a Texas A&M t-shirt and khaki shorts opened the door wide. When neither Elaine nor Jake spoke, he smiled.

"Yes?"

"Mr. Blanchard?"

"Yes?"

"I'm Elaine Randolph. My husband Jim and I bought your house over in Veil."

"Oh. Oh, of course, Miss Randolph. Come on in." He looked over his shoulder and called out. "Honey! Elaine Randolph is here." He held out his hand, grasping hers and pulling her across the threshold. "You all come on in here. And this is your boy?"

"Yes, this is Jake. He's doing a lot of practice driving these days. He turns sixteen in a few weeks. He's trying to get ready to take his driving test."

"Hello!"

Valerie Blanchard—a pretty woman in her mid-forties with a natural smile—burst into the entry. She threw her arms around Elaine in delight.

"Hello!" she exclaimed again. "I'm so glad to meet you. And this is Jake." She looped an arm around his neck and pressed her head against his. "How are you?"

"Good. I guess."

"What a surprise," Clay said. "What brings you all to Mt. Pillow? Practice driving?"

Elaine started to speak and stammered. Jake spoke up instantly.

"Money," he said. "Mom found a big sack of money in the attic. She wants to know if it's yours or we can keep it."

The Blanchard's looked at Jake, then Elaine.

"No," she said. "Honestly, we never got to meet at the time of the closing and I just wanted to come and meet you and introduce myself. If this isn't a good time, we can come another time."

"This is a perfect time," Valerie said, hugging her again. "Let's go sit in the kitchen. I just made some cranberry punch. It's wasted on Clay."

"We have some Coke too," Clay said to Jake.

"Cool. You have a really cool backyard too, the way it goes right down to the lake."

"Did you see the dock?"

"Dock? You have your own dock?"

"Couple of boats too." Clay looked at Elaine. "Okay if I take your chauffer down to see the dock?"

"If it's not a bother."

"It'll keep him from having to sample cranberry punch."

Clay disappeared down a hallway with Jake alongside. Elaine heard a door open and, for an instant there were the outdoor sounds of birds, cicadas and distant boat engines.

"Men and boys and their toys," Valerie said. She hooked her arm in the crook of Elaine's. "I'm so glad you came. I've been curious about you."

"You have, Valerie?"

"Val. Please call me Val. I hope it's all right if I ask how you're doing. Recovering from your surgery, I mean."

"They say I'm making good progress. Maybe you could tell, when you asked why we were here, I sort of zoned out for a moment. That still happens to me when I'm under stress."

Valerie pulled out a chair for Elaine and she sat down at a table overlooking Pillow Lake, lined with cedars and elms and shimmering in the midday sun.

"Hope you like this." She set a tumbler with ice in front of Elaine and poured it full of a red-purple punch. "I got the recipe on line. It's supposed to be good for your kidneys, and tasty too." She filled a second glass. "If it's poison, we'll die together in style."

"I love your place here, Val. The house in Veil is nice, but this is really wonderful. I can see why you would want to move here."

"Well I'm glad you like the place in Veil. It's not all that special. And I know you have a nice, nice home in Richardson. I'm just glad our little house worked out for you."

"Um. This is good. It was obvious to Jim and me that you took really good care of your home. It had lots of nice touches that we appreciated and wanted to keep, like the window treatments and the hardwoods in the hall and living room."

"Are you changing anything?"

"A couple things. We're moving the gazebo a few feet back so we can put a hot tub right outside."

"Ooh! That sounds nice."

"And we're painting the kids' bedrooms."

"Your girl couldn't take the lavender, huh?"

"Jake couldn't take it. The kids changed rooms."

"Really?" Valerie's expression gained the slightest curious, wary distance. "Why?"

All the sadness she had felt for Valerie and Clay reading the articles about the disappearance of their daughter flooded in upon Elaine. She felt as if she were about to weep.

"I made them switch rooms actually . . . when I found out about Nicole."

Valerie's smooth face darkened, suddenly lined with tears. She took the paper napkin from beneath her glass and wiped her eyes. Elaine watched her in silence.

"It's amazing. After all these years it still has the same effect on me."

"I cannot imagine how awful that must have been."

She nodded. "Beyond words. Beyond imagination. You don't even know what it does to you until you realize two or three years have passed and you're still not over it."

"Especially since . . ."

Valerie looked at her. "Especially since they never found her?"

"Yes. That's what I was going to say. Did they never find any real clue?"

"Never. Do you hate us? We were really torn about not telling you, especially since you had your own young daughter. Do you hate us?"

"No." She shrugged, then smiled. "Not at all. Janet explained it to us. Since no one really knows what happened, you can't be sure anything happened in that room. There's really nothing to tell."

"You're so kind. You're so kind." She patted Elaine's hand.

From just outside the back window came the roar of a boat motor. Momentarily a speedboat appeared, coursing across the water—Jake at the wheel and Clay perched beside him.

Elaine shook her head, then turned back to Valerie. "Is it okay for us to talk about this? Can I ask a couple questions?"

"Of course. I'll tell you whatever you want to know. It's the least I could do, especially since we didn't tell you about Nicole before you moved into the house."

"Is losing Nicole why you moved over here? Because you couldn't take being in the same house any more?"

"Well, yes and no. Clay is originally from Mt. Pillow." She sighed and took a sip from her glass. "For a long time he had been wanting to come back here. That spring when it all happened we had found a place here—not this place, but a nice one. We were ready to move, but Nicole didn't want to leave her friends. So we made a little compromise with her: we wouldn't leave until school was out. . . . If we had moved right when we signed the contract on the house, she would never have been taken."

"That's ironic, isn't it?"

"There's a lot of irony all around this. Weird, fateful things. You see, after she disappeared, I couldn't help but hold out hope that she was still alive. I mean, I knew in my head she wasn't coming back. But I just couldn't give up. You know what I mean. You're a mom."

"Yes."

"So once she was gone, we backed out of the deal to buy the house and move here to Mt. Pillow. We stayed there in Veil in that house, full of all those awful memories. Hoping against hope. Praying she would come back. . . . For, it must've been years, every night I sat on the porch outside her bedroom. We kept her room just like it was. I would sit in the porch swing where I used to sit and rock her when she was a tiny baby. It was right outside the window, the window I know someone took her from. . . . And every night I would say, 'Come home to me, child.'. . . But she never did.

"Finally we got to the place where the pain of losing her

outweighed the hope of her coming back. I had to . . . be realistic, I suppose. So after we waited six years and we knew she wasn't coming back—or at least it was terribly unlikely—we decided to sell the house and come here to Mt. Pillow."

"Is that why you got rid of her old playhouse, so you didn't have to see it every time you looked out in the backyard?"

Valerie smiled. "Exactly. I would see that little castle when I walked to the kitchen for my morning coffee and start crying. Then when I walked back to the bedroom to get ready for school, I'd see it again and here came the tears."

"I don't think I could have lived through that. I mean, sometimes I just want to throttle my little Camille. But, really, if anything ever happened to her, I don't know how I could go on."

"Clay and I got closer." She gazed down at the table, rubbing the wadded napkin in her palm. "They say the death of a child often drives parents to divorce, but it was the opposite with us. We leaned on one another. It gave us strength. Our families were right there with us too. Both sets of parents were very supportive. They always knew the right thing to say. And when not to say anything. Our neighbors were there for us as well."

Elaine started slightly. "Yes. We've met some of them. They seem really nice. It's a good neighborhood."

"We were especially grateful for the Daughtry's."

"Oh, the police chief and his wife."

"Well, he wasn't the chief then. I think he was a deputy or something. But the two of them came over all the time. Larry was able to keep track of the investigation. All the police were involved and he would tell us what they were doing."

"That must've been quite a comfort."

"Yes, even when the police eventually stopped investigating, the Daughtry's kept up their support. They were always there when we needed something."

"Actually I heard he helped when you put in the gazebo," Elaine said.

"Oh, yes. Guess I had forgotten about that. He did help. Mostly with the excavation and the landscaping."

"Landscaping?"

"It was nothing fancy. When we first put in the gazebo, Clay thought it would be good to have some Chinese holly around it. After a year or so, he got tired of getting stuck every time he tried mowing around it. Larry heard him complaining about it one day and just came over one afternoon and dug out all the holly bushes."

". . . Wow. That's amazing. Suppose he'll do things like that for us?"

Valerie laughed. "Maybe. He was awfully good to us. I think mostly it was because Susan was dating Avery."

"What?"

Her quick response surprised Valerie. "Well, Avery Maxwell—"

"The boy who took Nicole?"

"The boy who disappeared the night she did. And for all intents and purposes probably did take her. He was dating the Daughtry's daughter Susan."

". . . No kidding?"

"No kidding. In fact, she and Avery had been out on a date earlier that night."

Elaine nodded. "Which must be how they knew he was in the neighborhood."

"Yes. I suppose it was. I've always thought, since Avery had been dating Susan, the Daughtry's felt a little bit responsible for what happened to my Nicole."

Elaine crossed her arms against her chest. She drew a deep breath. "You know, I would just love to walk through your new house here."

# Chapter 5

She realized as they drew to within half a dozen miles of Veil that Jake was anticipating all the directions she was giving him.

"You know the way back to the house?"

"Sure. It's easy."

"All right, Solo Boy. Just drive carefully."

Elaine gazed out the passenger's window at the rolling country, going over and over her conversation with Valerie Blanchard. She had been so startled to hear that the Daughtry's daughter Susan had dated Avery, Nicole Blanchard's kidnapper, that she had forced herself to change the subject. Now, leaning back into the passenger's seat of the Nissan, she felt she had the leisure to put together all she had learned and try to understand it. Intuitively she grasped that all the disjointed truths—both from seven years ago when Nicole disappeared, and from three nights ago when the apparition of Larry Daughtry appeared in the middle of the night in her backyard—were somehow linked in an ominous way.

"What do I know and what do I just think I know?" she asked herself silently. "I know that seven years ago the Blanchard's daughter disappeared. The last place anybody saw her was in her bedroom. From that bedroom window, you can see the back of the Daughtry's house. I know that, the same night she disappeared, a boy named Avery Maxwell also disappeared. Avery had been dating Susan Daughtry, the teenage daughter of Larry and Sheila Daughtry. They had been out on a date that night and Avery brought Susan home."

She stared out the side window at the flat, dusty landscape. They were less than a mile from Veil.

"There are things about the disappearance nobody knows," she thought. "For instance, nobody knows what happened to either one of those kids. That boggles the mind. . . . I wonder if Avery had a history of harassing little girls? I wonder if the police ever talked to Susan Daughtry about what sort of person Avery was? In his photo he looked like a kid trying not to show how harmless he really was."

Elaine tapped her finger against her lips, a habit developed during her days of making diagnostic nursing decisions—a habit she had not exhibited since she had suffered the aneurysm. "There is that whole other list of things I know. Like, Chief Daughtry has an unquenchable interest in the structures built in my backyard. He helped build the Blanchard's gazebo. After that he did all the landscaping around it. And this week he came over in the middle of the night and dug around it—probably because he knew I was going to move it. . . . And why dig around it if we were going to move it? Logically because there was something we would discover if we moved it. And today, right where he was digging, the workmen found a deposit of sand, where no sand should ever have been. It was as if someone had something there and moved it. . . . And sand comes in plastic bags, so you could use it easily to fill a void, if you made one.

"But what is the connection between Susan Daughtry's boyfriend disappearing with little Nicole and Chief Daughtry digging in my backyard? And is it my imagination that he keeps turning up like a bad penny every time I try to find out more about this?"

"Check this out, Mom," Jake said.

They were coasting up to a four-way stop sign on the eastern outskirts of Veil. Sitting off to their left, partially concealed by a small billboard, was a police car.

"I wonder if that's—"

"Yeah it's him," Jake said. "He's the one with the Dodge Hemi, remember?"

"Well just make sure to come to a complete stop. And don't burn rubber through the intersection."

They stopped for several seconds at the sign. Jake eased through the crossroads and continued slowly.

"Burn rubber?" he snickered. "In your car?" He was gazing into the rearview mirror and his expression suddenly changed. "Oh, man! Uncool. What is he trying to pull?"

"What?"

"That police chief dude turned on his lights and he's coming up behind me really fast."

For an instant Elaine thought she was going to have a spell. She closed her eyes and drew breath deeply through her nose. She had to be in control of herself in this moment.

"I need you to listen to me, son. I need you to do exactly what I tell you to do. Nothing more and nothing less. Do you understand me?"

"Sure, Mom. What is this guy trying to pull? Why is he always on us? We aren't doing anything wrong."

"Pull over to the side of the road, put it in park and cut the engine off." As he followed her instructions, she continued, "Turn on the emergency flashers and roll down both our windows. Whatever he says to you, no matter how outrageous it may be, you answer him with one or two words and very politely." She looked out the back window at the police unit behind them, its blue lights strobing, the driver's door opening. "Yes, sir. No, sir. That's all you say. Tell me you understand and you'll do exactly what I said."

"Mom—"

"Tell me!"

"Okay. I will."

Elaine heard the door behind them slam and the heavy steps of Larry Daughtry approaching the driver's side of her car. Then he appeared, bending over at the waist, smiling the ironic, frustrated smile that a parent of a chronically naughty child might wear.

"Jacob James Randolph."

Again he was familiar with Jake's full name.

"Kind of rolled through that intersection back there, didn't you, son?"

"No, sir."

Daughtry leaned back in mock disbelief. "You don't mean to tell the police chief he didn't see what he just saw, do you?" He placed the citation book in his hand on the threshold of the window. "Now let's see that driver's license."

Jake fished his billfold out of his back pocket and removed the learner's permit—pretty much the only thing in the wallet. His eyes forward, he handed the permit to the officer.

"Hmm. Not exactly a driver's license, is it, son? You're still months away from taking your test—if you get there. You know that a moving violation prevents you from getting your license until you're eighteen, don't you?"

He was going to respond and Elaine knew it. She swiftly covered his hand with hers.

"If I'm not mistaken, Chief," she said, "you have to be convicted

61

of a moving violation."

The officer smiled broadly. "Mrs. Randolph. That brings me to the second offense your son is facing. Since you have not been released to drive, I'm pretty sure your being in the front seat doesn't qualify as having a licensed, adult driver in the passenger's seat. Driving without adult supervision and running a stop sign does not bode well for a young driver who's trying to get his license."

"Perhaps we should take this to a county judge over in Cochran and let him sort it out," she said, smiling but with the slightest hint of defiance in her voice.

Daughtry straighted so that his face could not be seen by those in the car. With his hands on his hips, he exuded a reflective air, as if considering what he wanted to do with the young lawbreaker Jake Randolph.

"I really don't have to write this ticket, you know," he said. Bending down again, he nodded, unsmiling. "This has to do with adult supervision more than youthful error. Honestly, I have to lay Jake's mistakes—and his ability to get a driver's license—at the feet of his parents. Well, clearly right now it's up to his mom."

Jake again started to speak. She squeezed his hand.

"How do you suggest we clear this up, Chief?"

Daughtry leaned his weight on the driver's window frame. "Normally, when drivers need a talking to, I put them in my unit and give them a good lecture, personally. In this case, though, the driver is a minor, not a licensed driver. This isn't really on him, as I say. Mrs. Randolph, why don't you come back and sit in my car with me and we'll discuss this like two adults."

Before Jake could react, she spoke up. "I'll be glad to, Chief Daughtry."

The chief turned and started back to his car.

"Mom," Jake whispered harshly, "I'm not letting you go back there with that guy. I'm the one he—"

"Listen to me, Jake! This isn't about you. None of it. It's about me. You sit right here in this car and don't move. I'm going to be just fine. If you try to intervene, you're only going to make it worse." She opened the passenger door. "Promise you will just sit here. . . . I said—"

"Okay. I promise. But I'll be watching in the mirror."

"Everything will be just fine, son."

Elaine stepped out of the Nissan and closed the door. The shoulder of the road dropped off sharply to the drainage ditch beside it. She had to lean on the car as she made her way back. It occurred to her that her flat, smooth soled loafers only made her situation worse.

The passenger door of the police car was heavy, but she got it open and slid onto the bucket seat. The interior of the Dodge was cold. The air conditioner seemed to be running full blast.

"Thank you for coming back to speak with me, Mrs. Randolph."

"What's this really about, Mr. Daughtry?"

He chuckled, staring straight ahead through the windshield at Jake sitting in her car. "As if you didn't know. Today you paid a visit to the Blanchard's, our old neighbors. I'm sure you were full of questions about the tragic disappearance of their daughter. Yesterday you went over to the library to look up information about the poor child's abduction and about the punk who took her."

Elaine gazed at him. She was awestruck and relieved in the same moment. How did he know she had been to the Blanchard's? He hadn't followed them. They surely would have noticed. There were so many things he seemed to know. How?

And yet confronting Elaine as he was had to be a clear indication that she was close to knowing something—or finding something—he didn't want to her to discover. If she confronted him outright with all the questions she had, then he would know everything she had learned, what she had pieced together. She must, she decided, reveal nothing to him.

"Why does it bother you that I want to know about a child being kidnapped from my house?" she asked. "Why didn't you tell us when we moved in, neighbor?"

He shrugged. "It wasn't my place to tell you," he said. "Anyway, that was a long, long time ago. Most folks in Veil would just as soon forget it ever happened. It's cruel of you to reopen old wounds like this, Mrs. Randolph."

"Are you telling me I can't ask questions about my own house?"

"I'm saying." He took a breath and calmed his voice just slightly. "I'm saying you're in a real good position here. You aren't going to be in Veil but for a few months. You can let us keep our ghosts to ourselves and we will be the best neighbors you ever had."

She waited for him to continue. "Or?"

"Well . . . You've seen what can happen. Here is a fine young fellow like Jake with a splendid future and a spotless record. There could be misunderstandings between him and myself. Or another officer. I bet he can have a smart little mouth at times, can't he? Never knew a teenage who didn't. Those adolescent attitudes can really irritate a peace officer. Maybe get him locked up over night in the county jail. Sometimes prisoners there accidentally don't get segregated according to age. Minors get left in with the hardcore types." He faced her. "I just want you to know, Elaine, that I want to look out for Jake. I want to watch out for everyone in your family. I just want you to help me do that, is all. I just want you to mind what is your business and leave Veil's old sorrows alone to heal. . . . I hope you understand."

She felt herself shiver and looked away from him. "I do understand. I'll pay very close attention to Jake's driving from now on. He won't be taking me anywhere that's dangerous or off limits. He won't be running any stop signs."

"That's good."

"Am I free to go?"

"Of course. Give my best to Jim, will you?"

"Yes."

She pushed open the door and held onto it to keep from sliding into the bar ditch. It took all her weight to close it. Jake was looking at her as she got back into the Nissan.

"Are you okay, Mom?"

"Yes. Start the car and let's go."

When they had pulled out onto the road, she asked him, "Is he following us?"

"No. He's just sitting there on the side of the road with his lights off." He glanced over at her. "What was that about, Mom?"

"A disagreement between Chief Daughtry and me."

"What kind of disagreement?"

"Jake, it doesn't concern you."

"Yeah, but he dragged me into it when he stopped me like that. That guy is no cop. He's a joke. He's just a bully and somebody needs to let the air out of him."

She snapped her head toward her son. "Listen to me. There is nothing a guy like that would like better than for you to try to teach him a lesson. Don't you know that's why he stopped us? He wanted to show me how easy it would be to get you worked up. If you react against him—just a smart aleck word or making a fist, he can do anything he wants to you."

"I can handle that guy."

"I know you're very good at marshal arts, son. You have a very colorful belt and all. But that guy was military police. His job was to subdue and arrest strong, well-trained young men who could defend themselves. He could hurt you badly. Even kill you. And that you raised a hand against him would make it your fault." She studied his face. "Don't forget that."

When he didn't reply, she asked, "Do you understand?"

"Yes. I understand, Mom."

She leaned her head back against the rest. "You have to promise me you won't let anyone provoke you." She closed her eyes.

He spoke after a moment. "What's the point of learning jujitsu if you can't kick somebody's ass?"

Elaine smiled. She could feel herself slowly beginning to relax. A sort of pride seeped into her consciousness. She had not suffered an episode. Not at the Blanchard's and not in her confrontation with Daughtry. Perhaps she was getting better, even though moving to Veil was exactly the opposite of the rest cure it was supposed to be.

Once more she looked out the window and felt the multitude of questions flood her awareness. How did Daughtry know where she had been? Yesterday he had known where she had gone even before she got there. Was he following her in some way that she and Jake could not detect?

Wait. There was one other possibility. What if somehow he was listening in to her conversations? She had told Julie about both trips. She had explained to Jake where they were going on both occasions. What if Daughtry could overhear what she was saying? But how? The second night in the house when Jim found her sitting and brooding in the kitchen, she had been almost certain she heard someone moving around. What if Daughtry had gotten in? What if he left some sort of listening device? That would also mean he had listened to her conversation with Jim. What had they said? What suspicions about Daughtry had she voiced?

A wave of awareness swept over her, a feeling like suddenly realizing her clothes were open, unzipped, and she had not realized she was exposed. Was it possible he was listening in on the conversations taking place in her home? That would explain how he knew where Jake was driving her. She shook her head. Surely she was giving him far too much credit. How could a person be a police chief and have his own life and still listen to a full day of conversations from his neighbor's house. Then it occurred to her: voice activated recordings. It was even possible for software to zero in on a particular word or phrase in a full day of recorded conversations. That would enable Daughtry to ignore all the extraneous interaction in her house and listen for any mention of his name, or Nicole Blanchard, or the gazebo.

As she reflected on the possibility, two ideas occurred to her. First, she had to test the possibility somehow. She had to find out if it were true that Daughtry was listening in. Second, if it were true, she might be able to use his snooping to her advantage, to convince him that she was going to drop the whole issue of Nicole's kidnapping. It would disarm his suspicions and free her. . . . Free her to do what?

And then there was the question of what would cause a man like Daughtry to threaten people in this way. What frightened him so that he would eavesdrop and follow and coerce innocent people to stay away? To stay away from what? He would only threaten her in this way if he truly had something horrible to hide.

An idea of how she would respond to Chief Daughtry began to formulate in her thoughts.

Elaine took her handbag off the floor from beneath her feet and pulled her cell phone from it. She slid open the keyboard and began to type a text message:

"I need a favor from you. Nurse to nurse."

"Are the children asleep?"

Jim came around the edge of the sofa and sat beside her before he answered. "They're both in their rooms. Cammie is probably asleep. I'm not sure Jake ever closes his eyes. It might interrupt his video game."

Elaine sighed. "There's something I have to talk to you about."

"Yeah?"

"I sort of had an awakening moment today. I think I haven't really been making the kind of progress I thought I was."

"Well, honey, we knew it was going to take a fair amount of

time. That's the whole reason—"

"I'm not talking about my physical recovery, or even my neurological recovery. I mean, I think I've been having these sort of paranoid delusions. It's totally strange to me. I never had anything like them before."

". . . What are you talking about?"

She sighed. "Well you remember when I told you I saw the police chief digging around my gazebo?"

"Vividly."

"Yeah, well. The further I get from that, the more I realize I was just hallucinating."

"You've been having more of those?"

"Not exactly like that, but I find myself imagining all kinds of crazy things about our new neighbors—that they are hiding things, that they are stalking me. Really strange things. Then I have days like today when I come to myself and realize it's all in my imagination."

"Do I need to take you back to see the doctor?"

She shook her head. "I don't think so. At the moment I've got it under control. If I get delusional and there's no reasoning with me, then I guess I will need help. Julie, my home health nurse, is coming to see me again the day after tomorrow. I'll talk with her about it and see what she has to say. I'm probably not the first aneurysm patient to go through something like this during recovery. There is a medicine the doctor prescribed for me that I can use to help with hallucinations if I need it."

Jim sighed, as if about to bring up a difficult subject. "So I have to ask you this. It's been on my mind, especially with you thinking we have strangers in our backyard. What about the gun? Is it still in the phone table on your side of the bed? Should I unload it and put it away somewhere, maybe somewhere you don't even know about. You know, so you don't shoot somebody during an episode?"

She smiled. "No, love. As paranoid as I am, I've never gotten the urge to shoot anybody. And I taped the key to the gunlock onto the bottom of my lamp, so the kids can't find it and shoot anybody either."

"I'm going to trust your judgment on that, E." He caressed her cheek with his fingertips, as he had become accustomed to while she was in the hospital, the top of her head swathed in bandages. "You know I will do anything for you, hon. All you have to do is say the word."

"I know." She nodded. "And I would do anything to protect you."

When Jake and Camille were nearly finished with their pancakes, she spoke up. "We need to dress this place up a little. Don't you think?"

Her son looked at her with an expression of distaste. "Mom, you can't complain about the way I painted my new room and then ask me to paint the rest of the house."

"I'm not talking about paint, Jakester. I'm talking about window treatments, accessories, wall art that looks like it belongs here more than to our house in Richardson. If we're going to be here for a year, we might as well try to make it home."

"I'd like a picture for my room, Mom."

"Okay, Cammie. I think you should pick it out."

"Where do they sell art in Veil?" Jake asked.

"I don't know. I do know that they have a nice strip mall in Cochran. There is an art and craft store and a gift shop. It's a half mile down from Wal-Mart."

"Yeah?" he responded slowly.

"Wal-Mart," she added, "where they have a big selection of video games."

"Why does he get a new video game?"

"And those 'Teen Society' books you like, Cammie. When was the last time you got a couple of those?"

"Yes! Can we take the twins?"

"Oh I don't think so. Jake will be driving and that might make Mrs. Short a little nervous. We aren't going to leave for another couple hours anyway, if you want to play with them this morning. I thought we could eat lunch there in Cochran."

"I have to call them," Camille said, jumping up abruptly and heading toward the phone in Elaine's bedroom.

Jake watched her leave the dining room. "Why is she going back there when there's a phone right here?"

"A girl needs her privacy."

"Mom." His voice was quiet. "Don't you think we're pushing our luck?"

"What do you mean?"

"With that police chief and all. If he sees me out driving again—
"

"Oh, no, Jake. It'll be fine. Chief Daughtry and I have a new understanding. I don't think he'll stop us today. And if he does, we'll just explain we're going shopping."

His face was full of skepticism. "As much as you warned me about that guy, I don't want to take any chances."

"I don't intend to take any chances either, son. I'm being honest when I say that he and I have an agreement."

"Well . . ." He was struggling to understand. "So he agreed to back off of us. I got that. What did you agree to do?"

She considered her words carefully. "Mind my own business."

Momentarily a broad smile emerged. "Can I get you to make that deal with me?"

"Sure. When you're twenty-one."

After she finished the breakfast dishes, Elaine unplugged her laptop and carried it to the gazebo. She made certain to keep her back to the yard and not to mention any of her search terms aloud. The internet session only took her fifteen minutes. She memorized the telephone number she had located and deleted part of her browsing history, the part that had nothing to do with curtains, tablecloths and sconces.

"After all," she muttered, "I'm leaving you here. Who knows who might check you out while we're gone."

Jake was in his accustomed driver's position when she locked the front door and made her way to the garage. His bravado posturing of two days before, however, had given way to a new confidence. Elaine buckled herself in and nodded and he backed down the driveway.

"You know, son, when we go to your Grandmother Lou's this weekend, you should ask your dad if you can drive."

He glanced toward her. "Seriously? All the way to Euless?"

"Yep. I think you're up to it."

They quit talking as Jake reached the corner and turned toward the twins' house. The police chief was standing in his own driveway, leaning against the back of his Hemi, watching them. As Jake slowed to make the turn, Daughtry broke into a grand smile and waved, the sort of greeting one gives to dear friends. Elaine smiled and waved back.

"Why are you waving at that guy," Jake whispered. "Like he's not going to fire up his unit and chase us down on a whim?"

"He and I have a new agreement," she said. "It's like I told you, son."

Elaine kept her expression as calm and passive as she could, given that her heart was pounding. She asked herself if the police chief knew what he just confessed to her: simply by standing and waving instead of stopping and harassing them, he had revealed his awareness that she and her children were taking an innocuous trip— going shopping and out to lunch. Clearly he knew she was not doing any more investigating into the disappearance of the Blanchard child. That was why he could wave and be casual instead of threatening. Now the question was, did he intend to demonstrate so clearly to her what he knew? Was Daughtry aware he had revealed to her that he had overhead her conversation, either with Jim the night before or with her children only two hours before? Was his wave actually another veiled warning: "I know everything you say. I know all your plans. Don't cross me."

There was another question gnawing at her as well. Just how did he know what she was saying? Was he able to listen in from his house with some sort of sensitive device? Or had he been in her house? Had he planted a microphone or even a camera. She shivered. A wave of distress, a feeling of violation washed over her.

The instant Jake pulled into the driveway, Camille flew out of the house, followed immediately by the twins. They spoke to Camille, all the while staring at her brother, who stared straight ahead, his lips pursed.

"She'll be back after lunch, girls," Elaine assured them.

As they headed toward the outskirts of Veil, Camille launched into the most animated version of eleven-year-old gossip. She described the awful school teacher the twins told her to avoid—but with whom she would probably be stuck for the whole year. The gross teenaged brother of a girl she had not yet met. The right shoes and clothes to wear to Temple Houston Elementary so she wouldn't stand out, but so everyone would notice how cool she was.

Her monologue continued until they pulled onto the parking lot of Wal-Mart, at which Camille grew silent, for a moment. "Oh. This is Cochran?"

They got out of the Nissan and walked toward the massive front of the store together. The glass doors slid open for them and they were greeted immediately by a short, elderly, portly man with a blue shirt and a sweet, welcoming smile.

"Welcome to Wal-Mart."

"How are you?" Elaine responded.

When they were out of earshot, Camille looked back at him and whispered, "He looks like Santa's little brother."

"More like one of the elves," Jake said. "Say, Mom, if you can't be a nurse anymore, maybe you can be one of the oldie greeters at Wally World."

"Uh-huh. I hear they're phasing their greeters out. Cammie and I are going to the book section to see if they have any 'Teen Social' books. Why don't you go try out some of their new video games. Maybe you can destroy a planet or something."

"How many can I get?" he asked. "Like two?"

"How much allowance do you have left?"

"Um. I guess I'll get one game. And you may have to help me a little."

"I see. Maybe we can work an advance on your allowance."

He smiled over his shoulder as he headed toward the electronics department. "I'm sure we can negotiate it."

"I know you're sure."

As they walked toward the book department Camille asked, "Why does he get everything he wants?"

"Like you don't?"

Camille spotted the teal-colored books in the mid-grade section instantly. "I don't have about half of these, Mom."

"Well, look them over. I figure three books is about equal to one of your brother's video games. And I'm guessing you don't have any allowance left either?"

"Allowance?"

"Right. Cammie, I'm going to stand over here and make a phone call. I'll be right here where you can see me, okay?"

Her daughter did not answer.

Standing with her back to the tabloids, Elaine slipped the cell phone from her purse. She recited the phone number she had memorized as she pushed the buttons. There was the faintest hum of telephone lines being accessed and then a ring. After the second ring, the call was connected.

It was a woman's voice, weary and interrupted. "Hello."

Elaine kept her voice low, so that no one around her could hear. "Hi. Is this Debbie Maxwell?"

". . . Who's this?"

"My name is Elaine Randolph. On Monday of this week my family moved into the house in Veil that used to belong to Val and Clay Blanchard."

". . . So what do you want?"

"Well I'll just put it right out there. When we moved in, we didn't know anything about what happened in that house before we bought it. But I've spent a week learning more and more of the story. I know your son got blamed for the disappearance of the Blanchard's little girl, but I really don't believe he did anything. I think there were two kidnapping victims and that your son Avery was one of them."

She didn't realize until she stopped talking that her heart was racing and she was holding her breath, waiting for Avery's mother to respond. The silence between them stretched to nearly thirty seconds. Elaine began to wonder if she had hung up.

"Why are you calling me about this?"

She took a deep breath. "Some strange things are happening around our house. Things that make me suspect Chief Larry Daughtry was involved in the disappearance of Nicole and Avery."

"That bastard!" The woman's voice was suddenly charged with anger. "He got in the way of the police investigation. He all came across as so innocent and acting like he was helpful. Nobody ever asked him about his part. Nobody ever questioned his word."

"You suspected him too?"

"He threatened Avery! He hated Avery. Avery was just a harmless boy. He never hurt nobody. But Larry Daughtry thought he wasn't good enough for his precious girl."

"Why didn't you tell the police?"

"Time I got to them, Daughtry had beat me to it. I tried to tell 'em Daughtry was bad and mean. Only he already had 'em convinced Avery had done something to the girl."

"I read the stories about it," Elaine said. "They didn't suspect Avery right away. They didn't even know he had disappeared."

"What happened is this." Her voice was adamant, the rage still fierce after all the years. "I went to the police the morning he didn't come home. But they paid not much attention to me. See, if a little girl gets stolen out of her bedroom, that's news. But a teenage boy, they just think he's off and up to mischief. So they didn't give me the time of day.

"Soon as I heard about the Blanchard girl, the across-the-yard neighbor of the Daughtry's, I knew in my heart the two was connected somehow. So I went back to the police. I begged 'em to quiz Daughtry about where he was. They told me, 'Deputy Daughtry has already come forward and made a statement.' For a minute I thought that meant he confessed that he had done something to Avery. But they kept talking around it in their cop way. Finally I realized that he had told them to make Avery a suspect. Said Avery was bad news. Said he had tried to force himself on Susan. Police never asked Susan if that was true. And they never interviewed me or Harley, Avery's stepdad at the time. They just took Daughtry's word 'cause he was a lawman."

"Nobody ever listened to you?"

"Nobody. TV people come around sticking cameras in my face, but they just played me up for poor white trash. They mocked me. Mark my words, they let the guilty man walk away scot free while blaming my child." Her voice broke.

"Mrs. Maxwell. Debbie. What do you think Daughtry did? And why?"

She had been crying and swallowed. "See. That night Avery had took Susan to a dance at the high school. I don't think they was out late. Avery was too scared of her dad to do that. But now my son did have a mouth on him. He would talk big sometimes. Something had to happen between the two of them. Avery was sure no match for him."

"How did Nicole Blanchard get involved?"

"That I can't imagine. But it makes me know it had to happen right there at the two houses. Nicole wasn't outside somewhere. It was her bedtime."

Elaine sighed. "If Daughtry kidnapped both of them, what did he do with them? The police tore up North Texas looking for them."

". . . I don't know. Whatever he did, he didn't go far to do it. Avery's old car broke down every couple hundred miles and he never had more than a quarter tank of gas. That's the thing. Even if you believed he stole the girl, my son didn't have no money and frankly not enough wit to escape with her. . . . Far as I can tell, everything points back to Daughtry."

She felt herself nodding. "That must've been a really bad time for you, Mrs. Maxwell."

"It was pure-D hell, I'll tell you. It was bad enough pining for my boy—and knowing that bastard killed him somehow, but everyone was blaming Avery for the little girl being gone. And when they blame the child, they blame the momma. Harley and me up and moved out here to Wichita Falls. After a time he left me too. He adopted Avery and raised him as his son, but when push come to shove, I guess he felt the need to give up on him and me too. Now I have no idea where he is either. . . . How'd you find me, by the way?"

"Computer. Internet search. You can track most anybody these days if you know how." She paused. "Mrs. Maxwell, I believe every word you're saying."

"What can you do about it? Nothing!"

Elaine shrugged. "Maybe not. If I figure it out, though, I will let you know. I promise you that."

# Chapter 6

Elaine met Julie at the head of the driveway just before she got to the front door.

"I have a big favor to ask you. Could you drive me to the drugstore? There are some personal things I need and I don't want to ask Jake to take me."

The nurse seemed uncertain. Or, at the least, surprised. "Well. Okay."

"I hope this isn't against your rules or anything," Elaine said, not hesitating to get into the passenger side of the car. "I promise it won't take any longer than the scheduled time for your visit and we can talk on the way."

Julie got back into the driver's seat and fumbled in her purse for her keys. Elaine sat back, her eyes closed. It was only after they had driven for a full minute that she turned and spoke.

"Were you able to get everything?"

"I did, actually. It wasn't easy either. This better not come back to bite me in the butt."

"It won't. I can promise you that. . . . Do you think I'm crazy?"

"Unfortunately no. I would be much less anxious right now if I did think you were loony. I'm worried for two reasons. One, you just might be crazy and I'm supplying you with what you need to reinforce your insane behavior. Two, if you're not crazy, then you're living next door to an extremely dangerous man who is really keeping close tabs on you."

"Well look at it like this," Elaine said softly. "If I am crazy, then what you brought me today will never be used."

"So you still think the police chief is spying on you?"

She nodded slowly. "Without following me, he knows where I've gone, what I've done and who I've seen. Then he does follow me. He shows up places where he knows I'll be. The day before yesterday he stopped us and told me exactly where we had been, who we had seen and what we talked about. I know he's eavesdropping on me. I don't know how he's doing it though."

"If you're so sure he's doing this, why haven't you gone to the county sheriff or even the state troopers? And by the way, do you really need to go to the drugstore?"

"Not really. I just needed to make an excuse. I don't know what the guy can hear and what he can't. Probably you should go ahead and drive me over there though. I feel so paranoid. But like you said, I've thought several times about going to other authorities. There are two problems though."

"Two?"

"Yeah. The first has to do with what Debbie Maxwell said to me."

"Who's Debbie Maxwell?"

"She's the mother of Avery, the boy who supposedly kidnapped Nicole Blanchard. Earlier that night he had a date with the chief's daughter Susan."

"Oh. That's interesting."

"Isn't it? Mrs. Maxwell tried going to the police to tell them her son was missing. She tried telling them that Larry Daughtry hated the kid and she thought he had done something to the boy. But Daughtry beat her to it. By the time she got the police to pay attention to Avery being gone, Daughtry had already convinced them that he had taken the girl." She shook her head. "If I tried going to the police, I know what Daughtry would say. 'Well, fellows, she has some mental problems. She has some spells. She sees things that aren't there and imagines all sorts of things. She found out about the little girl's kidnapping and realized it took place in her house and just went off the deep end.'"

"Well how would he explain his stalking you?"

She sighed. "That's the second thing. It's strictly his word against mine. I have nothing but suspicions, and frankly I don't know what I suspect him of. If I say he has followed me and eavesdropped on my family, it will only make me look crazy, because I can't even prove that."

Julie pulled onto the pharmacy parking lot, shut off the ignition and turned to her. "So then. What is your plan exactly? Why do you need this peculiar little bag of medical supplies?"

Elaine drew a deep, ragged breath. She shook her head and smiled. "I have no idea what supplies you're talking about."

Jim was clearly tired when he plopped down beside her on the sofa. He squinted at her, his expression doubtful.

"Headphones? Do those hurt your head?"

"No. My head isn't sensitive at all any more."

"You know, if you're going to hang with the styling kids, you have to go with ear buds. Headphones are so 20th century."

"Ah, I know." Elaine slid the headphones back so they slipped down her neck to her shoulders. "I tried the ear buds. They just weren't happening for me. Anyway, I hear the music much better this way."

"So I was going to ask about that too. You got an MP3 player?"

"Jake helped me pick it out. Then he spent all yesterday afternoon loading my music onto it. I have 427 songs and it isn't but half full."

"Um, Elaine, dear, I could really care less about your MP3. I'm glad you have it. I also notice you have some new pictures on the walls and—what do they call them—accessories sitting around here and there. Things I haven't seen. Jake is playing a video game that's a whole different kind of destructive violence from anything he had before. And Cammie went out of her way to show me her new awful pre-adolescent books. . . . It doesn't bother me that you bought those things. I just wonder how you did it. Did one of our new neighbors drive you around?"

She patted his hand. "Actually I got several rides from one of the safest, most attentive drivers I know."

"Oh my god," he said slowly. "You let Jake drive."

"Exactly. He drove me three times this week and did a great job. I was going to suggest that, tomorrow when you and the kids go to your mother's, you should let him drive."

He started to respond and suddenly his expression changed. "Me and the kids. You're going, aren't you?"

"No, honey. I'm staying here." She shook her head. "Nothing against your mom, but this has been anything but a restful week for me."

"But we promised her we would come."

"Sweetheart, I'm only talking about me. The rest of you go. She loves to see you. She even loves our kids, for whatever reason. I will consider it a personal favor if you just let me stay here and rest." When he didn't respond, she said, "Promise me you'll go."

"Do I have to promise I'll let Wonder Boy drive?"

She laughed. "No. He is a good driver, though."

Jim sighed. "All right. We'll go. Can't say I'm all that excited about leaving you here alone. If you have any problems, do you know who to call for help? I guess it's a good thing the police chief is our backyard neighbor."

The sudden darkening of her face caught his attention immediately. They stared at each other. He called her by her most personal, cherished name.

"What is it, E? What's wrong?"

"You know how I said a couple days ago that I had been having these paranoid delusions, that I had been imagining things about our neighbors?"

"Of course I do."

"So . . . I'm not having that sleeping problem where I don't know if I'm still dreaming. I think I'm past that now. And I've been thinking maybe the things I've been seeing are not my imagination after all."

"What do you mean?"

She dipped her shoulders, avoiding eye contact with him. "It was part of why I had Jake drive me places. I had him take me to the county library so I could read up on the disappearance of Nicole Blanchard. Then I had him take me to meet Val and Clay Blanchard."

"My god, E. To Mt. Pillow? What are you trying to prove?"

"I'm just trying to understand what happened. I just want to know why the police chief was in my backyard in the middle of the night."

"I thought you said that didn't really happen."

"Well it might have, Jim." There was a whine of protest in her voice. "It was very real to me. Even a person with a brain injury can see something that's wrong and out of place."

". . . So what have you discovered with all your 'investigations'?"

"I haven't—I haven't found anything definitive. But I have come up with a lot of real questions, questions that deserve an answer. These are questions you and I can't answer."

"Uh-huh. Well who can?"

"The county sheriff."

Jim's jaw dropped. "You want to go talk to the sheriff? You want to ask him to answer questions about an investigation that was closed six or seven years ago?"

She shook her head vigorously. "I don't think it ever was closed. They never found Nicole or Avery, the boy they say kidnapped her. So technically the case is probably still open."

He nodded slowly. "Probably? You think you have some information the county sheriff would be interested in?" Gradually his voice began to rise. "I'm guessing every lawman in Texas was searching for those two and couldn't find them. And you think the sheriff is going to start investigating again because you believe you saw the police chief digging in your backyard in the middle of the night?"

Elaine gazed at him, her expression meek.

He looked down. "I'm sorry I came on so strong. You aren't going to have an episode, are you?"

"No."

"Okay." He sighed. "Weren't you going to ask your nurse—"

"Julie."

"Julie. Did you ask her about this?"

"Yes."

"So what did she say?"

". . . Well, she's sympathetic. She says that brain trauma can cause false perceptions."

"Like imagining you see things?"

She nodded reluctantly. "That. And also there can be personality changes. She—she brought me that medicine I told you about. It's supposed to clarify my thinking. Just some samples of it is all she brought. If it works for me, she'll get me a prescription for it."

"I think you should try it."

Elaine leaned toward him, her hand on his. "I will. I promise. But there's something I want from you, and it's a big something. . . . Monday morning, I want you to take me to the courthouse over in Cochran."

His voice sounded weary. "Why is that, E?"

"Here's my idea: while you're at your mom's this weekend, I'm going to make a list of everything I know, of everything that's happened since we've been here, and of all the unanswered questions I have. I'll write it down and read it to the county sheriff. After I give it to him, it's not my problem anymore. It's his."

Jim responded slowly. "And what if he says there is nothing to this, that it's all in your imagination? What if he says there are rational explanations for all the concerns you have?"

"That will be that, then. I promise I'll drop it. But what if he does decide to investigate?"

He studied her face. "Well, it wouldn't be the first time you were right when nobody else thought you were."

She sighed. "Thank you. I love you."

"I love you too."

"I don't know how upset your mom is going to be about me not coming with you, but yesterday, when Jake took us over to Cochran, I did your mother get a present from all of us."

"No kidding. I had no idea Cochran had a Neiman Marcus."

"Ha. No. I happen to know she has a weakness for real tomatoes."

"Vine ripe?"

"Yes. I have a big sack of vine ripe tomatoes sitting on the back porch. . . . In that checkerboard suitcase of mine she always liked. I want her to have that too."

"Uh. Well that's very generous of you, E, but why would you give that away?"

She leaned forward and kissed him, smiling. "We should really take a nice relaxing trip, just you and me, before school starts. And coincidentally, I'm going to need a new suitcase."

# Chapter 7

This was not, she decided, Jim's favorite Saturday ever. As she stood waving, watching her car back out of the driveway, she could not help but notice the simple, closed mouth nod he gave her in return. That was all. The cool response, she knew, was one part worry about leaving her alone for thirty-six hours, one part wariness about Jake driving all the way to Euless and one part extreme reluctance to take her to see the county sheriff on Monday.

Still Elaine continued to wave casually, smiling happily as if to inspire confidence in Jim. And Jim was the only one looking at her. Jake, dark glasses obscuring his eyes, was all about demonstrating to his father the driving skills he had already proven to his mother, and could not be distracted by the mere cordiality of bidding farewell to his mother. Camille, in the back seat, was popping bubbles with multiple pieces of gum and intently reading one of her Teen Social books.

Elaine remained standing in the driveway watching until the car was completely gone from sight. Then, softly, she said, "I love you so much. Be safe."

She turned and went into the house and locked the door.

She heard something.

Despite wearing the headphones, she was almost sure there was a new sound somewhere in the house she did not anticipate. Holding the MP3 player in front of her, she tried to remember the right sequence of buttons to push. Then she moved her headphones back so they slipped down, encircling her neck. The noise was coming from Jim's study, the place where everyone used the desktop computer. The whirring sounded like the printer was initializing itself.

Did it periodically do that on its own and she just hadn't realized it?

She dropped the novel she had been reading on the bed beside her and stood up. Glancing at the clock—ten after midnight— she felt a growing wariness as she turned on the hall light. She leaned on the frame of the bedroom door for an instant, listening for any other sound.

It was only a half dozen steps to the study. Standing in the hallway, she felt along the wall inside the room and turned on the light. There was no one in the study and the computer monitor was dark. Still the printer, as if supernaturally possessed, began with its jerky motion to churn out a page. After it produced the single sheet, its sound and movement ceased.

Elaine stepped into the room and gingerly picked up the page that had emerged from the printer. She rolled it over and read the short paragraph silently:

*Dear Jim, Jake and Cammie,*

*I'm so sorry it had to end like this. I can't tell the difference between what I really see and what I imagine anymore. Please forgive me, I just can't go on.*

*Elaine"*

Her eyes flashed about her, to the open closet, to the open hallway door. She glanced back to the computer and realized the monitor's power button was black. The computer was on. Someone had turned off the monitor.

In the next instant the light in the hall died. She stared, panicked at the darkened doorway. The silence was broken by the calm voice of a man, the sound jolting her before she made sense of his words, just as it had the first time she heard him speak.

"Thank you so much for picking up that piece of paper, Elaine."

She felt herself tumbling backwards, her eyes rolling upward. But someone was catching her, preventing her from falling. There was the sensation of being carried in darkness and then placed in the light, of being gently stretched out on a soft place.

As quickly as it began, the episode ended. She could feel and hear herself breathing again. Eyes fluttering as she looked about herself, she realized she was lying back on her bed, her head resting on her pillow and the headphone cord tangled around her neck.

And sitting beside her—his feet on the floor, watching her, dressed completely in black—was Larry Daughtry.

"Back with us, I see. That was a bad spell. You were out for a good twenty seconds. I had to carry you and you were dead weight. But, even at that, you don't weigh much." He tugged at the leg of her pajama bottoms, his hands encased in plastic gloves. "What are these? Silk? The turquoise suits you. Picks up the blue in your eyes."

Elaine pulled away from him, edging toward Jim's side of the bed.

Daughtry laughed. "Relax. I'm not going to do anything sexual to you."

At last she could speak again. "Why—are you here? What do you want?"

"Just to dump out and close up the can of worms you decided to open." He brushed the disheveled hair from her face. "Wasn't sure how I was going to do it until you gave me this perfect opportunity— Jim and the kids gone for the weekend. Your family perfectly safe and happy. That leaves just you and me to get things settled."

"What things? What—do you want from me?"

"Oh darlin', don't you worry your confused little head about it. I've already got everything under control. And you've already done everything I need you to do."

"What—did I do?"

"Oh, you picked up your suicide note."

A wave of heat flashed through her again. She thought for an instant she would pass out again.

"Now your fingerprints are on it. When the county forensic folks dust it, they'll see you held it. Picked it up from the printer to proofread it before you left it on the kitchen table. That way you knew you wouldn't get blood on it."

She reached past him toward the lamp on her nightstand. Though she tried as quickly as she could, he caught her hand in his before she could grasp it.

"Now, now, darlin' that will never do. There isn't going to be a struggle here tonight. That's not part of the plan." With one hand he held her wrists together and picked up the lamp with the other. "Were you going to try to hit me with this? Maybe you intended to hit me first, but I bet what you were really going for is under the lamp."

Gently he placed the neck of the fixture across his legs and looked at the felt bottom. "Why look at that. Right where it's supposed to be. I believe that's the key to the trigger lock for your revolver, you know, the one in the drawer beside your bed. The one Jim should have put in a safe place, where you couldn't use it to take your life."

Tears coursed down her nose. "You can't get away with this."

"I already have, darlin'." Dropping the key in his shirt pocket, he set the lamp back on the stand.

"People will know I didn't kill myself. I wasn't ever suicidal."

"Oh, I don't know. With that awful head injury you have. With the back-and-forth between you and your husband about whether or not you were seeing things—ghosts in your backyard. Your home nurse will tell the investigators how much trouble you were having adjusting. Anybody could understand how you just couldn't deal with the confusion anymore. Then too there's your suicide note and your text message and your phone call."

"What are you talking about?"

He produced Elaine's sleek cell phone from another pocket. "They'll look at your cell phone record and see that, about ten minutes from now, you will have made a phone call to my personal cell phone. When they ask, I'll tell them you called to apologize for believing I was stalking you. Of course I graciously accepted your apology. If only I had known how desperate you were, I would have radioed for someone to come to your house immediately."

"I don't even have your cell phone number."

"Of course you do." He grinned. "I gave it to you when you sat in my car the other day. I told you to save it in your cell phone in case you needed it one day. As for tonight, I obviously couldn't prevent your suicide because, as the cell record will show, I was nearly over to Cochran when you called. Well at least that's where my cell phone is right now, in a safe place, programmed to receive the call I'm going to make to it momentarily and to remain online until your phone hangs up. It's a great alibi. Isn't technology wonderful?

"And here in—say—another five minutes or so when everything is finished and I'm getting ready to leave, I'm going to use your phone to send a text message to old Jim. It'll be brief and to the point. I figure that will help them fix the time of death."

She turned her face to her pajama sleeve to wipe her eyes and nose. "There will be marks on my wrists. They'll know you overpowered me."

"No they won't." A smirk crossed his face. "That was one of the great things about being in the military police. I picked up a few tricks here and there, like how to control people—even rough 'em up if I had too—without leaving a trace that I was there. Oh, by the way, I hope you don't have a latex allergy." He waved his hand before her. "Not even any fingerprints from me."

"Jim will never believe I did this. Even if you text him. Even with that phony note. He knows I suspected you and he won't let you get away with this."

He leaned down to her, his face right in front of hers. "For his sake, I hope he is wiser than you." He straightened. "Anyway, I'll be able to point to evidence I was nowhere near here when you gave in to your depression."

Elaine set her jaw. "You owe me!"

He looked at her skeptically. "Yeah, darlin'. And I'm about to pay you in full."

"No! If you're going to kill me, you can at least answer me."

"About what?"

She glanced about. "Well, how did you always know where I was going, who I was talking to?"

"Oh I have my little birdies here in your house. The night after you saw me digging under the gazebo and you started asking all those nosy questions, I knew I was going to have to keep track of you. So I snuck into your house. You heard me. Remember? You got up and eventually Jim got up too. I had been planting some listening devices around discretely. Voice activated. Top of the line toys. I have to say it was tough for me, just standing there behind your utility door as the two of you talked. But once I got the bugs planted, I was able to monitor everything that was said. That's why I was so surprised when you asked Jim to take you over to the sheriff on Monday. Hadn't you figured out I knew everything you were saying? I thought I had dropped enough hints—that I was clear enough about what I knew you'd figure it out. How could you not know I heard every word you said? If you did go to the sheriff, I was prepared for that. I might have come out of it all right, but it was a chance I just couldn't take. They might have opened an investigation on me. Did you think I was just going to let that happen?"

She studied his face. "What were you so afraid of? What were you digging out from under the gazebo?" When he didn't answer, she continued with a note of anger in her voice. "You killed both those children, didn't you?"

"Children." He snorted. "Avery Maxwell was no child. He was bad news on wheels. He was just a punk with nothing going for him. No plans. No ambition. He had the hots for Susan and, every time I tried to warn her about him, it just pushed her closer to him. Why is it innocent little girls like bad boys?"

He shifted beside her on the bed, looking away as he remembered. "Then the evening of that last dance he took her to, I bumped into Marlin Travis. He used to be a pharmacist here until he retired. I saw him at the diner around suppertime. He began to tease me that Maxwell had come into his drugstore that afternoon and bought a box of condoms.

"Well I don't have to tell you that got all over me. That night I was waiting, standing in the shadows by the cedar bushes where they couldn't see me when they pulled up in that trashy car of his. Susan thought I was off somewhere on duty. He walked her to the door. When he got back to the car, I was waiting. . . . When I confronted him about the rubbers, he got in my face. I guess he figured he had nothing to lose since I caught him and confronted him. Boy was he wrong.

"I just grabbed him by the throat and started telling him how he had seen Susan for the last time. Instead of laying still and listening, the little shit tried fighting back. Just like that I did him. With my bare hands. Just like I had been trained."

Elaine trembled as she waited for him to go on. "So why did you abduct Nicole?"

He shook his head in disgust. "Oh that's where it gets sad, darlin'. As soon as I realized he was dead, I got his keys and popped open his trunk and stuffed him inside. As I was closing it, I looked over to the Blanchard's house and sitting there staring out the window was little Nicki. Poor thing. She wasn't concerned at all. I don't think she had any idea what she was seeing, and I had no idea how much she had seen." He sighed. "But I knew she had seen something." He glanced at her and shrugged. "What are you going do? Cover up is always worse than the crime, they say."

". . . So what did you do?"

"Well, I came over to her window and tapped on it really quietly. She wasn't afraid of me at all. After all, she had known me all her life. She unlatched the window. I raised it, reached in and pulled her out and put my hand across her face and nose and held it there. . . .

Then I put the window back down and put her in the trunk with Maxwell."

"Here's a question for you," she said boldly. "What did you do with them? How is that no lawman in Texas could find either one of them."

He pulled the gunlock key out of his pocket and turned it over in his hand. "That was no big deal. I have a good size storage locker on the other side of town. A twelve-by-twenty. And I've got a chest freezer in it. You aren't supposed to access that storage facility after hours, but since I was a police officer, Harley, the owner, gave me a key. I drove Maxwell's car over there and pulled it inside the unit. I put the two bodies inside the freezer and walked back to where I parked my unit. Then I waited for things to die down, for the investigators to quit looking for them. The good luck of it was that they were looking for a pervert who kidnapped a little girl. Killing Nicki turned out to be a stroke of good fortune'""

"Debbie Maxwell was right about you all along."

"Oh, the kid's mother? Talked to her, did you? I seen her coming. I went out of my way to be helpful to the county and the state. I fed just the right information to the fellows."

"So they discounted everything Avery's mother had to say."

He nodded slowly. She could feel his grip tighten on her wrists.

"Same as I'm going to discount everything your boy Jake tries to say. Well, aren't you tired of asking? I'm pretty tired of answering, Elaine. Let's get this finished up."

"One last question. You do seem to enjoy boasting about all this—and who else can you tell?"

"Well you got me there. What is it?" he answered impatiently.

"Why were you digging under the gazebo Monday night? There had to be some reason you did that. There was something that incriminated you."

He nodded. "It was Nicki. She's been under there for years." He sighed. "After a couple months, when the search died down, I took a police department wrecker in the middle of the night and put Maxwell's car on it covered in a tarp. I put the kid's body in the front seat. I took it over to Lake Texoma and put it on a house boat and took him right out to the middle of the lake and dumped him there. Good riddance, I say.

"But I didn't have it in me to get rid of Nicki that way. It was pretty heartbreaking to know that Val and Clay were still pining for her. Eventually they came up with the plan to replace her little swing set with a gazebo. That was where I saw my chance. I helped set up the gazebo and all the while I was making a little coffin for Nicki. A tiny little thing, just her size. I thawed her body and put it in lime in the coffin. And when the time was right, I dug a place under the gazebo and put her there. . . . All that time Val used to sit in the little girl's room and say, 'Come home to me, child.' I bet I heard her say it a thousand times. And Nicki was right outside under the gazebo all along." He laughed. "Plus, if her bones were ever found—what's left of them—it would look like Clay did it."

"Where is she now?"

Daughtry frowned at her. "'Cause of you—your hot tub and your inquisitiveness—she's back in my storage shed. I didn't want to chance the construction boys finding that little coffin. Don't worry though. I'll figure out somewhere here around your house to bury her again. Shouldn't take too long. Your family will probably move back to Richardson after your funeral. Nothing to keep them here."

He squeezed the key in his hand and looked down at her. "You understand, Elaine, this is nothing personal. And if your family stays out of my business, I promise I'll protect them as long as they live here."

She sighed. "I would try to appeal to your morality or your humanity, but I've about decided that's a waste of time."

He chuckled. "Yes, times a wasting. If I'm not mistaken, the lock this key fits is on a loaded revolver right inside this drawer."

Daughtry lifted her hands a little higher, as if to demonstrate he wasn't going to let go and leaned toward the nightstand. He pulled open the drawer and slid his hand inside. Instantly he recoiled, pulling forth his hand and holding it before his eyes. Three hypodermic syringes protruded from it, one in the palm and two in the back.

"What the hell!"

Elaine caught her breath. "How about that. Got you with all three of them."

Daughtry started to stand, trying to figure out what had happened to him and how he should respond. His body began to shudder and, as if in slow motion, he crumpled and slumped to the floor, releasing one of Elaine's arms. With her free hand she reached beneath Jim's pillow and produced a nickel plated revolver.

"Is this the gun you were looking for?" she asked. She put the barrel against his head. "Looks to me as if the trigger has already been unlocked."

Helplessly he lost his grip on her other wrist. Incapable of voluntary movement, he settled into a jumbled heap.

"That's the first thing you have to learn about those latex gloves, Larry," she said, standing up. "They're very useful for a lot of things, but they won't stop a prick. . . . What? No clever comeback? No pathological threats? No arrogant boasts? Cat got your tongue?"

She stepped across his motionless body, set the pistol atop her dresser and opened the top drawer. "Probably you're wondering what I injected you with. Secsal Coline. Fast, isn't it? You probably won't die—even though you got a triple dose of it. I was trying to make sure I got at least one injection in you."

She produced a bag of sliding plastic fasteners and sat down beside him on the floor where she could look into his eyes. "The drug prevents voluntary muscle movement. Usually it doesn't stop your heart or your breathing." She tilted her head. "I'd really hate that because, frankly, I'd be really torn about performing CPR on a miserable murdering bastard like you.

"And what about that delivery system, eh?" She nodded toward the nightstand. "Those jump injectors are so cool. Not meant to be used that way, but in a pinch they really work. What was that you said about technology?

"But the thing about this drug—" She laboriously rolled him completely onto his back. "—is that it not only takes effect quickly, but it wears off quickly. So I have to hurry you see."

She pressed one of his wrists against the opposite ankle, looped a thick plastic tie around them and cinched it tightly. "Left to right and right to left." She repeated the process with the other ankle and wrist. "I think this is going to be awfully uncomfortable for you. But honestly I don't care. I think about those two dead children in Avery's trunk, and in the freezer in your storage unit. Really, I don't care how contorted you are. However—"

She yanked on his belt pulling him next to the bed. She lifted one leg to the bed frame and fastened it just above the knee with two plastic ties. She looped a tie through the back of his belt and around the bed frame.

"—Since it is theoretically possible that you could run with your off-hand-on-either-foot, I'm just going to make sure that you have to take my bed with you if you do."

Elaine sat down heavily, staring into the pale, blue eyes that gazed back at her. She pulled the headphones from around her neck.

"Now I know what you're thinking, Larry Daughtry. You're thinking that this is all your word against mine. Even lying there helpless and all, you're concocting what you want to say when the police get here." She tilted her head to the side, regarding him with curiosity. "So you'll probably say, 'She lured me over here. Check her phone records. She called me and I came immediately. I just happened to be all dressed in black like a ninja. She tricked me into reaching into the drawer and then she trussed me up and called the police with this fantastic story.'"

She wrinkled her nose. "That doesn't explain away the dead body of a little girl in your storage unit, does it? You'll probably say I found it while digging around the yard and put it in there to frame you." She shrugged. "Knowing you, you'll think of something a lot better than that, won't you? And you are so persuasive.

"You're problem is you tend to underestimate people, Larry. Of course I knew you were listening when I told Jim to take me to the sheriff on Monday. I was counting on you trying to stop me." She dangled the MP3 player in front of his face. "You're not the only person with a recording device, you pompous dumbass. Did you know that MP3 players are also recorders? When I heard the printer running, I turned on the record function. It's been hanging around my neck the whole time recording every word you've said."

Swinging the little device, she bumped it against his nose. "I got it all right here, Larry, inside this tiny little thing: your confession to two murders and one attempted murder." She got onto her knees, leaning toward him. "And you know the great thing about these digital recorders, dude? You see that little USB port there? You just plug that into your computer and download what you recorded. Then you can send it as an email attachment.

"Guess what, Larry? That's exactly what I'm about to do! Yep. Before I call the police, I'm going to email this digital file to everybody on my contact list. That includes my hubby. Boy, it will be so nice to say to Jim, 'I told you so.' And it also includes Valerie and Clay Blanchard. They're going to hear in your own voice how, every time they went out into their gazebo, they were standing over the bones of their little daughter, who you murdered so she couldn't tell anybody about the first murder she saw you commit.

"Also on my contact list is Debbie Maxwell. I wonder how she'll feel when she hears you confess that you killed her son with your bare hands because you didn't want him having safe sex with your daughter." She stood and looked down at him. "You know, this is just a guess, but I don't think things are going to go so well for you."

She stepped across him. He followed her with his eyes and she realized his voluntary muscle control was returning.

"I guess I'll take my gun with me. Just in case you somehow get loose. And, Larry, I suspect that tonight wasn't the last time you're going to get some injections you don't want."

# Chapter 8

"I thought the preacher did a good job."

Valerie Blanchard turned to look at Elaine in the backseat. "Yes. I thought so too. Especially since the deaths happened so long ago and he didn't know either Nicole or Avery."

"It was outstanding when you consider there's a murder prosecution going on and he was doing the funeral for the victims," Clay said, his eyes fixed to the road, attempting stoicism despite evidence of the tears he had not been able to resist throughout the memorial.

"And I thought the news media people did a pretty good job of keeping their distance," Elaine went on, nodding as she looked out the windows at the quiet neighborhood. "Especially after the service. Nobody stuck a microphone in our faces."

Valerie smiled. "I heard that was your doing."

"Mine?"

"Uh-huh. I heard you said you would grant exclusive interviews to networks that left us alone."

"After the trial. I said I wouldn't grant any interviews until after the trial. And I said I wouldn't talk now or to anybody who pestered any of us before the funeral was over. . . . I just don't want to say anything out loud to prejudice this case before it gets resolved."

His voice soft, Clay said, "I heard there may not be a trial."

Elaine glanced toward him. "Oh?"

"That's what we heard from the county attorney's office, Elaine," Val responded. "They said Daughtry's attorney was looking for a plea to save him from the death penalty. The CA put an offer on the table: two consecutive life-without-parole sentences for the murders, then twenty-five years after that for the attempt on your life."

She thought it over, asking herself how she felt about it. "Wonder why they didn't mention it to me?"

"Well we asked them what they were going to do," Clay replied. "They probably would've told you if you had asked."

". . . You're Nicole's parents. What do you think of it?"

Clay and Val looked at each other.

"I just want it to be over," Clay said.

Val nodded. "Me too. Executing Daughtry won't bring Nicole back and now there's finally a resolution to my child's disappearance—that is, there will be on the day he's sentenced. And I never thought there would be. . . . And I'm so glad you're safe. What an incredible risk you took."

Elaine smiled. "That's what Jim keeps saying. Only not in such a nice way. The alternative was to give in to a bully who I figured was a criminal. I wasn't going to do that. When Jim starts in on me, I just say, 'Honey, in my position, you'd have done the same thing.' He hasn't come up with a good come back to that one yet."

"Speaking of your husband—" Clay gazed in the rear view mirror. "—he sure has a serious look on his face back there."

"Oh, I know about that," Elaine said, grinning broadly. "He's still trying to get used to Jake always wanting to drive everywhere—and Jim has no good reason to say 'no.'"

Looking out the rear window, Valerie said, "We have quite a little entourage following us back there. I think almost everyone from the cemetery is coming to your house."

"Isn't that strange?" Elaine replied. "It must feel like they're coming to your house. Well today it belongs to all of us."

"I'm sorry Susan Daughtry didn't come to the graveside. I was real glad she came to the funeral though." Val began to weep again. "I think she felt bad about what her father did."

Elaine nodded. "And I think she really cared for Avery. I think she felt bad about what happened to him. Maybe she felt responsible."

"Was anybody surprised that Sheila wasn't there?" Clay asked.

"I'd have been surprised if she was." Val sniffed. She dug in her purse for a tissue. "She must've been terribly embarrassed."

"I haven't seen her at all since the arrest. She just stays in the house with the blinds drawn."

Clay shifted in his seat. "The story in the neighborhood was always that Larry was so controlling Susan couldn't stand him. She moved out as soon as she was old enough that her father couldn't stop her. And she wouldn't come back. She made Sheila go over to visit her."

"How could Sheila have lived with that guy so long and not

know what he was like?" Val asked. "Do you think she suspected that he had killed Nicole?"

"And how about that little spy room of his?" Clay looked over his shoulder. "Did she honestly think all that surveillance equipment was necessary for a small town police chief?"

Elaine shrugged. "For me to pull off what I did, I had to simultaneously deceive both my husband and Daughtry. But that was a one time deal. How can you fool someone you're married to for all those years?"

"Oh it happens." Val's eyebrows arched. "Some people deny obvious truths for a lifetime. And Daughtry was such a good liar. All that time the police were investigating, Clay and I were absolutely convinced he was the best friend we had."

"I kept telling him how lucky he was," Clay said, "that Avery hadn't done anything bad to Susan."

As they turned a corner and the Daughtry house, shuttered and still, came into view, they grew silent. Irresistibly they all turned and looked toward the gazebo in Elaine's backyard.

". . . So I wanted to tell you," Elaine spoke up, "that Cammie moved back into Nicole's room. I had her move out, you know, when I heard what happened. But after the—arrest, Cammie said there was no reason for a girl not to have the best bedroom. So I let her move back in. Jake had painted it an awful, depressing 'boy' sort of color. But Cammie made him help her repaint it. It's not the color you left it. It's a real dainty yellow. But at least you can tell it's a little girl's room again."

They pulled into the driveway of the house that used to be the Blanchard's, but now—at least for a time—was the Randolph's and parked behind Jim's Buick. A stream of cars pulled up one by one, lining the street around the house. People emerged and began to walk toward the front door.

"You two go on in," Elaine ordered quietly. "The door is open and there's stuff to eat. I'm going to stay out here and welcome everybody as they arrive."

She stood on the driveway, her hands folded in front of her.

Jim stopped and kissed her as he and their children walked past. "I am proud of you, you know."

"That's good to know, sweetie."

"That doesn't mean I'm ever going to forgive you," he said as he walked toward the front door.

Close behind him was the heavy set figure of Debbie Maxwell, wearing what was surely a brand new and very attractive black dress. She meant to speak when she stopped and grasped Elaine's hand, but the handshake became a hug and the intended words became tears. The two stood holding one another and crying for a time, well wishers slipping past them into Elaine's house for the reception.

"I can't thank you enough," Debbie said at length. "Thank you for bringing Avery back to me."

"I'm glad they found him, Debbie. I was worried the car would be covered with silt and the divers wouldn't be able to see it."

She nodded vigorously. "God wanted him found. That's why He brought you here." She sniffed and wiped her nose on a hanky. "If it's okay, I'm going to go in and use your ladies' room."

"It's the first door on the left as you go down the hall."

"Hey you!"

Elaine turned back to find herself face to face with her home health nurse. They embraced one another silently.

"So I was right. You weren't crazy."

"You were also right that I was living next to the most dangerous guy on the block. You're my favorite nurse, girlfriend."

"Um-hmm. Just out of curiosity, did anybody ask where you got those drugs and injectors?"

"Actually they did. One of the deputies who was here that night asked what I had used to drug Daughtry and where I got it." She shrugged. "I told them I was a nurse and I had that medicine for a long time. He dropped it at that."

"Did he think nurses keep syringes and paralyzing drugs just lying around?"

"Oh, wait!"

Tim Starling had started to walk around them quietly on his way into the house. Elaine stopped him with a hand on his arm.

"Julie, this is Tim. Tim, this is Julie." She opened her hand toward Tim. "He's the contractor who has relocated our gazebo and is installing our new hot tub." She opened her hand toward Julie. "She's my home health care nurse."

"Oh." He grasped Julie's hand, smiling at her. "You must be the one who got her the paralyzing drug."

The women stared wide-eyed at each other, astonished.

Elaine shook her head. "Tim, Julie has no idea what you're talking about," she said firmly.

"Whatever." He smiled at Julie. "Shall we go in and cruise the refreshments?"

"Yes." Her voice was bright. "I'll be right there. I need to set up my next appointment with Elaine."

"Okay."

Together they watched him walk into the house and close the door behind him.

"He's cute," Julie said.

"He plays the trombone."

". . . What's that got to do with anything?"

"Nothing. I just thought you'd want to know he's musical."

"How did he know about the—"

"I have no idea. I can assure you I have not mentioned that to anyone. It does sound like other people have been talking about it though."

Julie sighed, her lips pursed. "Well here's what I think. It was a real embarrassment for the police—local, county and the state—to have one of their own caught trying to kill somebody in cold blood and confessing to killing two children. I think they just want this to go away. As far as they are concerned, the fewer questions they ask, the better."

"That's probably why they are so willing to plead Daughtry out. They're going to let him plead guilty to two murders and an attempted murder. A trial would show how he manipulated people into ignoring evidence and ignoring important questions from people like Debbie Maxwell."

Julie nodded. "Well I'm going in and see what looks tempting on the table. You?"

"Yeah. Looks like every one is here. I'm coming in."

As they turned to go into the house, Julie spoke quietly. "I think I failed you as a nurse."

"Well I think you saved my life. What are you talking about?"

"I was supposed to help create this peaceful environment where you could gradually recover from your brain injury."

"Yeah. And Veil was supposed to be this harmless, sleepy little town. Maybe I was doing better than anybody thought and I really didn't need to come here."

"Maybe you're just a very resilient person." Julie held the door for her patient. "I've been thinking that some angels somewhere, or maybe the ghosts of those children, wanted you to come here and get justice for them."

They stood just inside the door, the laughter and conversation of her guests muffling her words as Elaine said, "You impute too much to me. I think it had more to do with a battle of wills. I've never liked bullies."

Julie nodded and tilted her head toward the food-covered table in the living room and the man loading shrimp cocktail on a plastic plate. "What's his name?"

"Tim. Tim Starling."

"Nice. See you tomorrow."

Elaine surveyed the hallway, living room and kitchen. There were at least two dozen guests spread throughout. It was clear from the timbre of their voices that the general atmosphere was tranquil. Though she had been introduced to nearly all of them—relatives and friends of the Blanchard's, classmates of Avery and even two or three from his mother's family—the entire crowd was virtually unknown to her.

Standing straight beside the laden table as if waiting to be recognized, wearing an apron with the slogan, "Don't Hug Me ' Til You Taste The Food," was her realtor, Janet Thomason. Elaine walked to her and embraced her.

"It is so good of you to put on this spread. I think there's enough food here to feed an army."

"The pleasure is all mine. I've been wanting to do something for you and Jim ever since you moved in. Especially after I broke the news to you about little Nicole."

"Well you didn't have to do a thing, Janet. But we appreciate it so much. And this is great. I notice everyone is staying close to the table."

"Swedish meatballs. Gets 'em every time. . . . So, Elaine, if this is not too soon to ask, will you and your family be staying here in Veil after this?"

"Just the kids. Jim and I are so tired of those snot-nosed brats. So we're moving back to California and leaving them here."

"I certainly understand," Janet retorted without a hint of a smile. "They can be so demanding. That's why my husband and I shipped ours off to an orphanage as soon as they were potty trained."

"An orphanage? Now that's a possibility. There would need to be lots of forced labor and bad food."

"Oh yes. Why the little homesick letters I get would make you want to cry."

At that Elaine broke into laughter. "You are too calm, Janet. Nothing rattles you."

"In my line of work it's self-preservation."

"Well look, we've been talking about what we're going to do and we just don't know yet. We can't get back into our home in Richardson for almost an entire year. We wouldn't mind staying here, but we don't know how the kids will be treated. If they aren't pariahs among the other kids on account of what their mother did, we'll stay here. If it's too difficult, we'll put the house on the market and rent an apartment in their old school district."

"I'll—"

"Yes." She put her hand on Janet's arm. "You'll be the one we call. We will definitely list with you."

The hint of an ironic smiled crossed her face. "Great. And I didn't even have to get you to try the artichoke dip."

She grasped her hand momentarily and looked around the room. "Will you excuse me? And when Jake shows back up at the table, just tell him I said to lay off the shrimp. Let everybody else have a chance."

Elaine walked through the room, gradually becoming aware that she was looking for Valerie Blanchard. She stopped at the sliding patio door, looking out across the back yard, the posts that would support the deck and the hot tub protruding from the jumbled earth. Val was sitting in the gazebo, gazing toward the street.

She opened the sliding door and made her way around the outline of the deck to the gazebo. Stepping inside, she sat down quietly.

Even without turning around, Val seemed to know who had joined her. "How strange. All those years I sat outside her window and called for her. 'Come home to me child.' . . . All the while she was only a few feet away. Every time we came out and sat in the gazebo. . . She was right beneath our feet."

"Well. . . now you'll know where she is, Val."

She nodded slowly. "She can rest now. And we can rest." Val

looked over her shoulder. "What about you, Elaine. Seems like life doesn't turn out like you'd expect for anyone who lives in this house. What's next for you?"

She drew a deep breath. "Well. . . . Six months after I stop having episodes, I can apply to get my driver's license back. I'm thinking I may regain more capacity than they said I would. So when I get my driver's license, I think I'm going to get my nursing license back."

"I think that's good. You'd make a wonderful nurse."

"Yes. I think I would. And if that doesn't work out, I may become a detective."

# A Whiff of Murder

*This bonus story, written by Lazarus Barnhill, centers around Detective Bob Vessey, whose tale is told in the novel The Medicine People, also published by Second Wind. For the purposes of our readers here, suffice it to say that Vessey has been removed from the police force of the small eastern Oklahoma town Okweekgo. After a stint in an alcohol rehabilitation clinic, Vessey is trying to make a living as a private detective in Tulsa, Oklahoma. Middle-aged, wiser, sober and cynical, Vessey hasn't lost his touch in examining crime scene evidence.*

His client's house was the last one on the last street of the subdivision. All the houses were pretty much the same—one story brick with a bay window to one side of the front door. Sometimes the window was on the right. Sometimes the left. The trim paint was different house to house. The brick color was different. He could see as he drove down the street that some of the houses had fenced back yards. But it was obvious they were all built from the same basic design.

An alley ran behind them, so each house had a rear entry garage. Thus Vessey was somewhat surprised to see Mrs. White's squatty economy car parked in front of her house—with her sitting inside it, staring at her front door.

Vessey parked behind her and got out of his brown Taurus. It wasn't like the Crown Vic he had driven all those years before he got kicked off the force, but at least it was a car he could get into and out of.

His client—still buckled in her seatbelt—was leaning against the inside of the driver's door, her gazed fixed on her house. She would've been a pretty girl, Vessey thought, if not for the work clothes she wore and her dishwater blonde hair pulled back in a careless ponytail. That, and her expression of utter dread.

"Here I am, Ms. White."

She nodded toward her front door without looking at him. "He's in there, Mr. Vessey."

"Your husband?"

"Yeah."

He studied the small façade for any clue that someone might be inside the home. "How do you know?"

"'Cause Delbert turns off lights," she replied. "Ever since he moved out, when I go to work at night, I always leave two on where I can see 'em when I get home. One in the entry. Another in the great room window. He's big on turning off any light I leave on. If the lights are off, I know he's in there. And they're both off."

Vessey produced his cell phone from his pocket and keyed in a number.

"What are you doing?"

"Calling your land line," he said, pressing the phone to his ear. "If he's in there watching for you, by now he knows we're out here watching for him. Maybe he'll answer. 'Specially if he doesn't want to get in trouble for violating the restraining order."

The phone rang twice. Three times. A fourth. Vessey heard the answering machine kick on.

"Hi, this is Cara. Please leave your name and number and I'll return your call as soon as possible."

"How 'bout it, Delbert," Vessey said loudly. "We know you're in there. Come on out and let's talk."

He closed the phone and slipped it back into his pocket. A minute passed. There was no sign of life from the house.

"Well," Vessey said, "why don't I go ring the doorbell?"

He had taken a couple steps when she spoke, her voice low and wary. "He has a gun, Mr. Vessey."

He turned back toward her. "A gun?"

"Yeah."

"What kind of gun?"

"Like—a pistol."

"What kind of pistol? An automatic or a revolver?"

"A revolver, I think. The bullet holder goes around."

Vessey smiled. "How long is the barrel?" He glanced at the house again.

"Short, I guess. Two or three inches."

"That's good. He'll have to get a lot closer to shoot at us." He produced his phone again.

"Now who are you calling?"

"The cavalry." He pressed the phone to his ear. "Just for future reference, Ms. White, if you think someone is inside with a firearm, don't sit in front of the house. Go to an alternate site and call for help—Yes, 9-1-1, we need police at 4729 East Spring Creek Terrace. We believe Delbert White is inside his domicile in violation of a restraining order and in possession of a pistol. . . . Yes, ma'am. Robert Vessey. I'm a PI employed by the wife of the subject. Yes, ma'am. . . . In front of the house . . . No. Haven't seen him." He closed the phone and put it away.

"Are the police coming?"

"Yeah. Just stay behind me, so Delbert can't see you from the house."

"He could shoot you."

Vessey smiled again. "He's not interested in me. You just need to stay put where he can't see you. If he really is in there. You didn't go down the alley to see if his car was in the back, did you?"

"No. I didn't need to. When I saw the lights off, I knew."

"Could be he went in, turned out the lights and then left."

"Why would he do that?"

"To accomplish just what he's done—creep you out."

She made a snorting, chuckling sound. "Delbert isn't smart enough to play a trick."

Vessey sighed. "Funny I don't remember you mentioning anything about a weapon when we were going through the peace bond process."

"I know. . . . I'm sorry. I was afraid if I said I had it, the judge would make me give it up, you know, so Delbert couldn't get it and use it against me."

"You mean, just like he has?"

"Okay. I should've said something. I kept thinking he was going to break in one day while I was sleeping and I'd wake up with him standing over my bed. I kept the gun right there for my own protection."

"And Delbert knew you had it?"

". . . He gave it to me for my birthday a few years ago." She laughed. "He always said he wanted me to be able to protect myself."

The police unit came from the short end of the street, from the narrow road that wound through undeveloped land and eventually drew near Mingo Creek and the Tulsa County line. As it pulled toward them, he heard the familiar, powerful rumble of the

Interceptor engine.

"Good quick response," he muttered.

The officer pulled the nose of his patrol car directly up to Mrs. White's vehicle. He glanced at Vessey and then, as he reported his location over his radio, he trained his gaze on the woman. He was a young man, strongly built with his light hair cut short on top and nearly shaved on the sides.

"I bet he's a reservist," Vessey thought aloud.

The officer turned off the motor of the cruiser and stepped out. He was an inch or two taller than Vessey. Confidence saturated the air about him like an overabundance of cologne.

"You Mr. Vessey?"

"Yes."

"I'm Officer Shaeffer."

"Thanks for your prompt response, Officer. In accordance with state law, I need to report to you that I am a licensed private investigator and I am carrying a concealed piece."

"Okay." He seemed totally unconcerned.

"I work for Mrs. Cara White. She's here in the car." Vessey stepped away from the driver's door.

"Ma'am."

His client's voice was full of relief. "Thank you for coming, Officer."

"Yes, ma'am." He straightened and looked back at Vessey. "What is the situation?"

"A couple months ago Mrs. White employed me to track down her husband, Delbert White. At that time there were a couple domestic violence complaints against him and Mrs. White was trying to serve him with divorce papers. We managed to locate the subject and serve him." Vessey shifted and took a half step toward the officer. "Because of the subject's history of physical abuse perpetrated against Mrs. White, we also managed to get a restraining order."

He motioned toward the house. "My client has reason to believe the subject is inside. She works third shift and always leaves multiple 'tell' lights on in the house. This morning all the lights were off. She believes the subject is inside the domicile and also that he is armed with a short barrel revolver."

Officer Shaeffer turned to the woman. "You were right to call us, ma'am. And your investigator has handled this properly." He leaned toward the driver's window. "Ma'am, may I have your house keys please?"

Vessey watched, lips pursed, as the woman pulled the dangly key ring—adorned with ornaments and grocery discount mini-cards—from her ignition and handed it to the officer. Shaeffer turned toward the house and Vessey fell in beside him as he walked across the street.

"A couple things, Officer Shaeffer."

"Yes sir."

"First off, I'm a retired peace officer."

"I know who you are, Mr. Vessey. Everyone on the force does. You're sort of—a legend all over northeast Oklahoma."

"That was nice, the way you said that." Vessey grinned. "'Specially since the Okweekgo department forced me to retire. Anyway. The other thing. I understand there were a number of domestic calls to this house. Did you happen to work any of 'em?"

"I ran a couple as I recall."

They reached the sidewalk and started toward the door, watching closely for any movement.

"Did he strike you as a guy who was just predisposed to violent behavior?" Vessey asked.

"Mr. White struck me as an ignorant redneck. His grandpa beat his grandma. His father beat his mother." They stepped onto the narrow porch. "He just carried on the family tradition."

Shaeffer knocked hard on the door. They stood silently, waiting, listening.

There was a thin glass panel on the handle side of the door. Vessey bent down and gazed through the tinted glass into the entry of the house. He heard the officer's voice.

"Well, let's go in."

He was still looking through the glass when the jangling key ring appeared beside his head. Shaeffer slid the key into the deadbolt. Vessey stood up and looked at the officer with a curious expression.

The door swung open quietly, revealing a barren entry that opened on the left side into a large room.

"Mr. White?" the officer called. "Tulsa Police. We're coming in. Empty handed."

Vessey was beside the policeman as they stepped into the great room. They saw Delbert immediately, slumped to one side in a recliner that faced them. The .38 had fallen from his hand to the floor. There was a small, neat spot on his right temple. The left side of his head from his ear backward had exploded outward and much of what had been within was strewn in a long oval pattern on the carpet beside the recliner.

The two men glanced at each other.

"Ever worked a suicide?" Vessey asked.

"No. I did two tours in Iraq though. This ain't shocking." Shaeffer walked to the unlittered side of the body and put two fingers on his throat. "He's dead."

"Looks like you got two jobs now."

"Two jobs?"

"Call for the coroner and some back up. Then you have to go talk to Ms. White."

"Me? You're her PI."

"She doesn't pay me for this, Officer. This is part of your job."

A smirk crossed the young man's face. "And what are you going to do while I do my two jobs?"

"Stand right here. If I'm outside when the forensic folks get here, they won't let me back in. If I just stay here, I'll become part of the crime scene."

"Crime scene?"

He nodded. "Suicide's against the law, Officer."

As he turned toward the front door, Shaeffer chuckled.

Vessey took a step toward the bay window. He watched the policeman walk down the driveway, key the mike of his radio and turn his head to the side as he spoke. He stopped on the near side of the street, conversing with the dispatcher. Seconds later he released the mike and walked to the driver's side of Cara White's car.

Vessey could see the young woman's face. She nodded. Even at twenty yards he could see the tears begin to flow.

Pulling the cell phone from his pocket, Vessey punched in a number and held it to his ear. It rang only once. "Captain Dunbar."

"Ronny? This is Bob Vessey. You working?"

"Always."

"How fast can you get in your cruiser and make it to East 4129 Spring Creek Terrace?"

"East? Christ. That's on the other side of town, Bob."

"Yeah I know. It's out in the boonies. How long since you ran lights and sirens?"

"What's up?"

Vessey considered his words. "Well. I really think you should be here for this. Listen to your radio. You'll hear the call."

"Okay. . . . 4129 Spring Creek Terrace. East."

He closed the phone and slid it into his pocket. Quickly he began to scan the room. He found the first item he was looking for in seconds.

A single sheet of stationery lay on a telephone table beside a lamp. Scrawled across the paper were two handwritten sentences:

*I'm sorry for all I did. I'll never hurt my wife again.*

Vessey read it twice. "Bet a million dollars that's Delbert's handwriting," he said, shaking his head.

He pulled the large Tulsa phone book off the bottom shelf of the table and placed it carefully on top of the suicide note, covering it completely.

Vessey took a breath and looked back out the bay window. The policeman was still standing at the driver's side of his client's car. No other official vehicles had arrived.

"Okay," Vessey said, "one down and one to go. Got to be around here somewhere close." He studied the room. "Sofa cushions."

Pulling the backrest cushions off the couch, he turned them in his hands. He found what he was looking for on the back corner of the middle cushion—a small, round, seemingly insignificant hole.

"Bingo."

He replaced the cushion and stepped back to the big window.

Two more police cars were parked in front of the house, the officers standing and talking to Shaeffer. The black crime scene van pulled into the driveway as Vessey watched. Police officers and a forensic tech began walking toward the house.

The technician, a balding, chunky African-American, smiled at him as he came in the door. "You Mr. Vessey?"

"That's right."

"Ha! Greg Shaeffer said not to move you. You're part of the crime scene."

Vessey laughed. "Not the first time for me, Slim."

"Is everything the way you found it?"

"Except for the stuff I moved around."

Now the tech laughed. "I got to take some pictures."

"Well you best stand over here," Vessey pointed to the right of the recliner. "This is definitely Delbert's good side."

"Oh yeah." He opened the lesser of his black equipment cases. "Aren't you the fellow was down in Okweekgo?"

"Twenty-six years."

"Heard you were good at crime scene."

"That was my job."

"So—" He pulled out a nice digital camera and stood up. "— what do you think of this one?"

Vessey shrugged. "Looks pretty cut-and-dried, doesn't it? A despondent husband—facing criminal charges, a divorce plea and kept away from the woman he obsessed about by a restraining order—takes the quick and least painful way out. And manages to get the last laugh on his ex in the process."

"Well." The tech was assembling equipment and making notes. "That seems to be the case. Only—" He trained the camera on Delbert's body. "—what I've seen—and I've only been doing crime scene for six years—what I've seen? Things that seem obvious often aren't exactly the way they look at first glance."

"Really?"

As if on cue, Shaeffer and two other patrolmen appeared in the great room.

"Hey, Officer Shaeffer, you're just in time. I was having this conversation about forensics with—I'm sorry, I didn't catch your name."

"Eddie Cook."

"Eddie. We were debating whether or not there could possibly be any explanation for this guy being dead here with his brains blown out other than that he's a depressed moron who committed suicide."

Shaeffer seemed taken back. "Well, is there?"

"I can't think of one." Vessey shrugged. "What about you, Eddie?"

The question surprised him. "I'm not saying there is any other explanation. I'm just saying you can't go on appearances. In a suicide like this, there are things you have to verify in order to rule

107

out any other possible explanation."

"Like what?" Vessey asked.

Eddie looked down at the body in the recliner. "Well, obviously, you'd check the right hand of the deceased for GSR. I mean, there has to be some gunpowder on his hand if he fired the weapon. If there isn't, somebody else shot him."

"Ha," Vessey crowed, "I can guarantee you 100% there will be gunshot residue on his hand. What else?"

"Well." The tech took a breath. "In my experience, when a guy kills himself over a girl like this, he usually leaves a note. Sort of a bad way to get the last word, but that's what they do. A suicide note lends a lot of credence to the idea he was killed by his own hand."

"Anybody see a note?" Vessey asked. "Don't touch it if you do."

He watched Shaeffer from the corner of his eye as the policemen and tech began to spread around the great room and adjoining kitchen and dining room. Shaeffer took a step toward the telephone stand and saw the phonebook. He stopped instantly, cutting his eyes toward Vessey, who did not look back at him.

"No obvious note?" Vessey called. "Maybe you'll find it in his car or somewhere. So Eddie. Any other way to determine for sure it's a suicide?"

"Oh." The tech stood with his hands on his hips, head down. "Well, the best way is to rule out the possibility that anyone else was here at the time of the incident. If he was alone, it has to be a suicide."

Vessey nodded. "Well, his wife was at work, just finishing up the third shift when he killed himself. Who else could've been here?—Oh, hey Captain."

The uniformed officers all turned toward the entry, startled at the appearance of their superior.

"Hey, Bob." He glanced at the others and the body of Delbert White. "What's this all about?"

"We were just having a conversation about crime scene evidence. We were hypothetically trying to determine if this could've been anything but a suicide."

"Yeah?" The captain's voice was skeptical.

"Eddie here—who by the way is very thorough—said the first thing to do is to check the dead man's hand for gunshot residue." He glanced at the young policeman, who watched him warily. "Of course, if you found GSR on Delbert, you wouldn't check anyone else for GSR. Unless you had a reason to. . . . So Officer Shaeffer, why would you have GSR on your hand?"

Everyone looked at Shaeffer.

"What?"

"GSR," Vessey said. "Why do you have gunpowder on your hand?"

Shaeffer stared back at him.

Vessey looked toward the captain. "Interesting, isn't it? He didn't immediately deny that he had gunshot residue on his hand, because he knows you're going to check for it now. He's not saying anything. He's trying to figure a good reason that he would've discharged his weapon recently."

Vessey glanced back at the tech. "What was that second test, Eddie? Oh yeah. A suicide note. Did you happen to see what Officer Shaeffer did when we started looking for one?"

"Uh, I—"

"He started over here." Vessey went to the telephone table. "Then he saw the phone book instead of—" He picked up the thick book by its edges. "—this suicide note. You see, if he had found it, he would've picked it up. That would've explained why his fingerprints are on it. Right, Officer?

"I saw this note here when Shaeffer went out to talk to Ms. White," Vessey continued. "I covered it with the phone book—but I didn't touch it. And about this note. I thought it sort of read funny." He glanced down at it. "Says, 'I'm sorry for all I did. I'll never hurt my wife again.'" He looked up at the silent men. "Now a fellow like Delbert was totally obsessed with his wife. If he killed himself and left a note, it would've been for her eyes. Only, this note doesn't talk to her. It talks about her."

They all waited for him to continue. Shaeffer's face was pale.

"Why would you write a note that says, 'I'll never hurt my wife again'? Sounds like he was making a promise. It's the sort of thing you'd write if a man was holding a .38 to your head. . . . Isn't that right, Greg?"

The silent group turned to the young policeman, who alone stared at Vessey.

"Now, there was a third key element to proving suicide, wasn't there, Eddie? Oh yeah, 'no other people present'. If Delbert didn't kill himself, somebody else had to be here. No evidence of that, is there? Well, maybe there is."

Casually he moved to the sofa. "You see, if I were going to stage a crime scene and I was a smart cop—like Officer Shaeffer— I'd know the forensic people would check the gun hand of the deceased for GSR. No gunpowder, no suicide. It would mean someone else was in the room and it would ramp up the investigation."

Vessey picked up the center pillow and turned it upside down. "Since Delbert wouldn't have shot himself twice in the head, a person staging the suicide would need to put the weapon in Delbert's hand and squeeze off a round. Then he'd open the cylinder, take out the first spent round and replace it with a new cartridge. Right, Greg?

"Now he'd have to do it without moving the body, which could easily be detected. He'd have to discharge the piece into something portable that would absorb the round, contain it and show no easily visible sign." He walked toward the tech, rolling the cushion toward him and pointing out the tiny hole. "Eddie, if you cut open this cushion, I predict you'll find a .38 round that came from the piece on the floor by Delbert's hand."

The captain spoke quietly. "Eddie, check his right hand for GSR."

Shaeffer sighed. "You don't have to, Captain. . . . He's right. I capped the sonofabitch."

Dunbar nodded to another of the officers, who produced handcuffs and touched Shaeffer on the shoulder. Head down, the policeman put his hands behind his back.

"Why, son?" the captain asked.

"He had it coming. He beat her constantly. I answered three domestic violence calls at this house myself."

"And you fell in love with the girl," Vessey said.

"Hey!" Shaeffer exclaimed. "I want to make this clear that this was all me. She has no idea I did this. . . . Sure, I fell for her. I wanted to help her out. She was never going to have a moment's peace as long as he was out there. But like I say, she knew nothing about this."

"Wrong," Vessey replied. "There are only two possible reasons you would've been here at the exact time Delbert was here. One, you staked out the place constantly until that one morning he finally does show up. That's more unlikely than 'true love.' Two, you lured him here. But how would you do that? He sure wouldn't come here to meet you. On the other hand, suppose Cara asked him to come. Suppose she called him last night—a very late hour, so he wouldn't have a chance to tell anyone about the call—and told him she decided to try to work things out with him. Suppose she said she was getting off an hour early, that she had left the back door open for him. Only, when he got here, you were the one waiting. She had to have conspired with you. How else did you come up with her .38 to put in his hand?" He nodded at Eddie. "Check Mrs. White's cell phone log. See if there wasn't a call from her to Delbert last night."

His head hanging, Shaeffer's voice was defiant. "He was going to kill her. It was only a matter of time."

"No he wasn't," Vessey said. "Six weeks he stayed away. No contact at all. He paid attention to the restraining order, Greg. I knew this guy. I followed Delbert and studied him. You were right about him being an ignorant redneck. He didn't know any better. He was holding onto the hope that, if he did what the judge told him, Cara would recognize he was capable of changing."

Shaeffer glared at him. "I did what I had to do to keep her safe."

"Safe? You were trying to keep her safe?" Vessey said incredulously. "I'm not trying to excuse the way Delbert brutalized her—don't get me wrong. Only he never killed anybody, did he? She was going to end up with you—a cold-blooded murderer."

Capt. Dunbar spoke up, "As you take Officer Shaeffer out and put him in the back of a unit, fellows, take Mrs. White into custody immediately. Don't give her any time to think about driving off."

He stood beside Vessey watching out the bay window as Shaeffer was led from the room where the body of the man he executed still slumped in the recliner. They watched as one of the policemen went to the car where Cara White sat—driver's door open, her feet on the pavement—and motioned for her to rise. He cuffed her hands behind her back and set her down gently in her car.

Dunbar shook his head. "Lost her husband, her lover and her future all in a couple hours. On account of making one phone call. Tough day."

"You know, that was truly amazing." It was Eddie, the forensic technician, who was still photographing the room. "I heard you were good at crime scene, Mr. Vessey, but that was incredible."

"Yeah." The captain's voice was weary, grudging. "That was remarkable, Bob. What put you onto him?"

Vessey shrugged. "There were several little things that sort of triggered my 'deception detector'. Like the surprisingly quick response to my 9-1-1 call. Shaeffer knew he had to stay real close so he would be the first one here. Then the two of them acted as if they'd never met, but when I asked him, he told me he had been here on several domestic calls before. He even knew that Delbert's father and grandfather had been wife beaters. I also picked up on the way he didn't have to go through all the keys on her crazy key ring. He picked out the right one right away. But you know how I knew he did it?"

"How?"

"I smelled it."

"Smelled it?"

Vessey laughed. "Part of my probation agreement—when they booted me off the force at Okweekgo—was that I had to go through rehab. Twenty-eight days. I decided I was not only giving up booze, but smokes as well."

Dunbar looked at him skeptically. "Yeah?"

"Well when I quit smoking, my smeller came back. I had no idea all the things I wasn't smelling. This morning, my head was down and I was looking through the glass right beside the doorknob when Shaeffer opened it. His hand was right beside my face and I smelled the cordite on him."

"You smelled the gunpowder on his hand?"

"Yep. Surprised the hell out of me. But I knew right then what we were going to see when we came through the door."

"So you're saying," Eddie spoke up, "you actually got a whiff of murder?"

"Yeah. I guess I did."

"Eddie is right, Bob. You're amazing at crime scene. You should come work for me on the Tulsa force."

Vessey chuckled. "Can't, Ronny. That's another provision. I got my retirement and probation, but only if I promised never to work as a cop again. Of course, I can consult on all your cases. Frankly, I need the work."

"What?  A smart PI like you?  You mean you're not rolling in the dough?"

He sighed. "Nope.  I just got my client arrested for murder.  You think she's going to pay me?"

# About the authors

Sally Jones, long an aficionado of murder mysteries, at last steps forward to try her own hand. In her first effort she has penned a cozy, engaging novel of suspense that readers will not want to put down. Though she has written for years, Jones finds the effort and concentration required to write a seamless mystery both exhausting and exhilarating. The professional administrator and paralegal is now developing a second thriller.

Lazarus Barnhill, a veteran novelist known for work that crosses genres and captivates readers, has melded his distinctive writing style with that of Jones in this, his first collaboration with another author. After a three year absence from the literary scene, Barnhill returned in 2012 with two new novels, as well as participating in the multi-author thriller *Rubicon Ranch*.

# Also from Lazarus Barnhill through Second Wind Publishing

## The Medicine People

After 25 years as a fugitive, triple murder suspect Ben Whitekiller returns to his small eastern Oklahoma hometown. Why has he come back? Why are those who sought him so disturbed at his return? What secrets will Dan Hook, the young officer who tells the story, find out about Ben, and himself?

## Lacey Took a Holiday

A desperate act of love creates a cascade of changes. Lacey, the most unlikely heroine, has been betrayed and abused by the men in her life. Andy has lost everyone he ever loved tragically. This 1920s mountaintop romance breaks every rule.

www.ingramcontent.com/pod-product-compliance
Lightning Source LLC
Chambersburg PA
CBHW071323130626
46556CB00004B/1717

# My Fair
# MASTER

## Gay Erotic Romance
## GIDEON ELLIOT